VAMPIRE FOR HIRE

PARANORMAL TEMP AGENCY
BOOK 3

MOLLY FITZ

ABOUT THIS BOOK

Something's up with the Paranormal Temp Agency, and I'm going to find out what that is. For my last two assignments, the cat boss Mr. Fluffikins had to drag me in kicking and screaming. This time around, I'm all too willing to play their little game. It's high time I learned why they plucked me from my ordinary everyday life and thrust me into this crazy new world filled with danger and magic.

But it's not going to be easy. Especially when the PTA orders me to help resident vampire Connie investigate a new coven that's just popped up in our sleepy little town of Beech Grove. For this mission, they grant me temporary vampire status—and all the perks and the punishments that come with it.

The real kicker? If we don't solve this one soon, I could be stuck as an immortal monster forever...

But that's just how it goes when you're a part-time vampire.

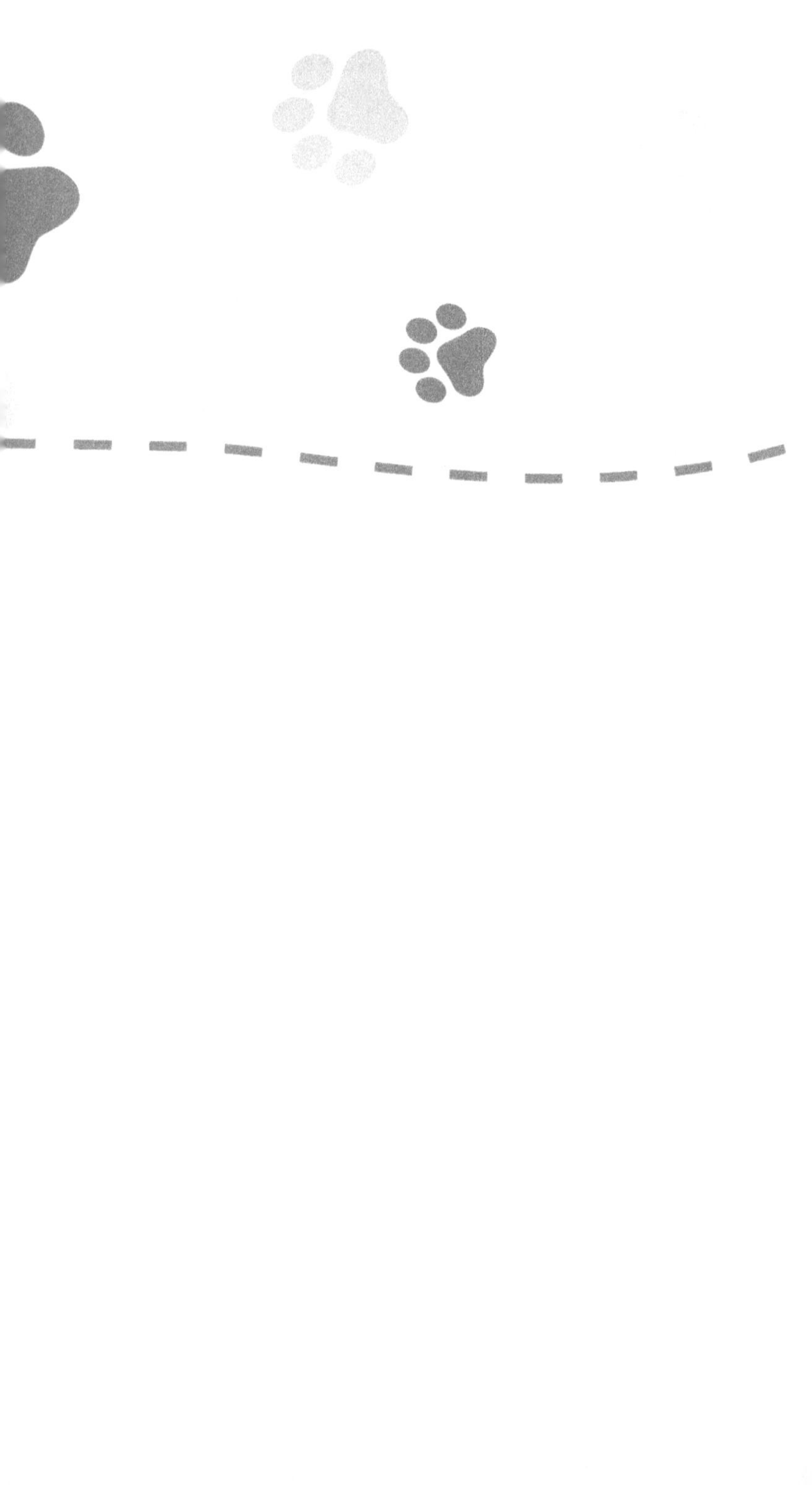

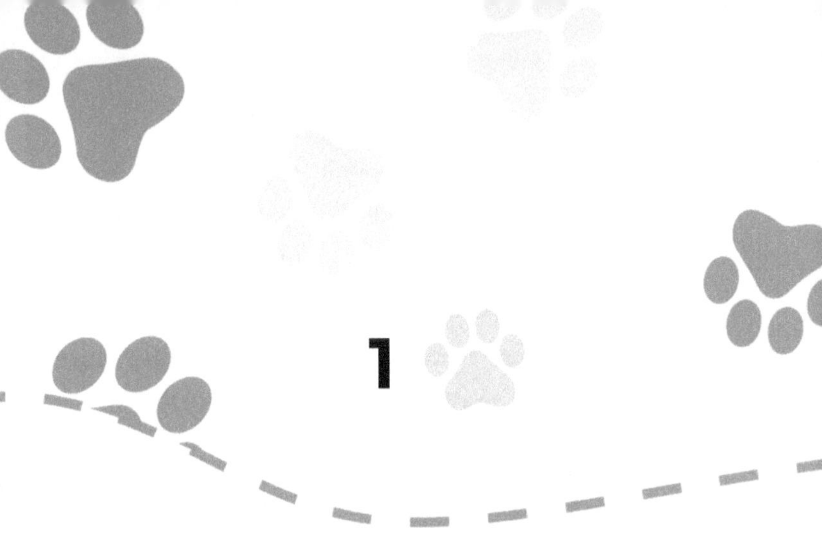

1

My name's Tawny Bigford. I used to think the most interesting thing about me was that I write romance novels part-time to make my meager living... But then I met a little black cat who changed everything.

His name? Mr. Fluffikins.

His role? Diplomat in charge of the local PTA. That's Paranormal Temp Agency, by the way—not the other organization that goes by the same unfortunate acronym. Just trust me when I say I have a fairly sordid history with those other guys.

Cough, cough. Cheating ex-husband.

Anyway...

Even though Fluffikins and I just met and I never asked for a job, he hired me as a temp and forced me to work two cases over the past week. The first was the murder of my former landlady. The second was a string of abductions that led us all the way to an island off chilly and scenic Maine.

I almost died at least once—and probably more—which might make it seem weird that I'm ready and eager to take on another assignment.

Let me back up a second here so you better understand the choices I've made.

The first thing you need to know is that magic is real. Seriously!

We're all born with it, but most lose it along the way. I had a brief taste of that special brand of power on my first case, and I've been craving more ever since.

But even though I know about magic, I'm not part of the community. I'm an outsider, what the others derisively call a "normie." Real magical folk are referred to simply as magicks. And the aforementioned PTA is a special governing body that protects their interests in our fair Peach Plains region of Georgia. They are but one of many such boards set up all across the globe.

There are seven permanent members of the board. Anyone else they need to work joins briefly as a temp.

Like me.

Usually temps get their minds wiped once they've served their purpose, but for better or worse, I remember everything.

The big boss is the bureaucratic black cat, Fluffikins. He is joined by the Town Witch, a role currently filled by my smoking hot neighbor Parker Barnes. I think we may be dating now, but we haven't kissed again since that first time almost a week ago, so who really knows…

Anyway, after Parker and Fluffikins, we have the five board liaisons. Greta is an honest-to-goodness angel who oversees the Schools. Connie is the cranky vampire in charge of Commerce. Then there's Buckley in Agriculture and some old dude in a suit for the Cemeteries. I know almost nothing about either of them.

We're supposed to have a liaison for the police force, too, but that position was recently vacated due to an unfortunate string of events that would take way too long to explain here…

So instead we have an intern who is applying to be the provisional liaison, if only she can prove herself worthy of the job. I don't have high hopes, considering she tried to kill me—and almost succeeded.

Yeah, I'm really not a fan, and that feeling is definitely mutual.

If you had asked me a week ago, I'd have told you I hate the PTA and want nothing to do with them. But our last big case made me spin a one-eighty.

There's something the others are hiding from me, something important, something about me. And I won't rest until I get some answers.

Last time, they dragged me to the local Paranormal HQ against my will. This time I'm going to show up at their door and demand their attention.

Our first two adventures also taught me something far more mundane. Namely, that it's hard to survive in this world without a car. So much for shrinking my carbon footprint, because I used my last royalty check to purchase a ten-year-old sedan to help get me from point A to point B.

The last two times I visited PTA HQ, Mr. Fluffikins had flown me there with his magic, but I liked being in charge of my own transportation this time.

And I arrived almost as soon as I'd pulled out of my driveway, given the old office complex that houses the PTA sat just a couple miles past downtown Beech Grove.

The windows hung dark, but I knew that was just a ruse to keep outsiders away. And magic or not, I was part of this now. At least that's what I kept telling myself as I gathered my carefully prepared package into my arms and marched up to the front door.

It was locked, so I knocked.

When no one answered, I grabbed a rock and smashed it through the glass door. Tiny shards flew everywhere, but I didn't care. I needed a way in, and it's not like they couldn't fix my little oopsie with a bit of well-placed magic.

What I had to say was just too important to wait. Hopefully I could find someone who was willing to not only listen, but also to speak.

I'd been their pawn up until this point, but now I was ready to be a stronger player in the game…

Just call me "Bishop Tawny."

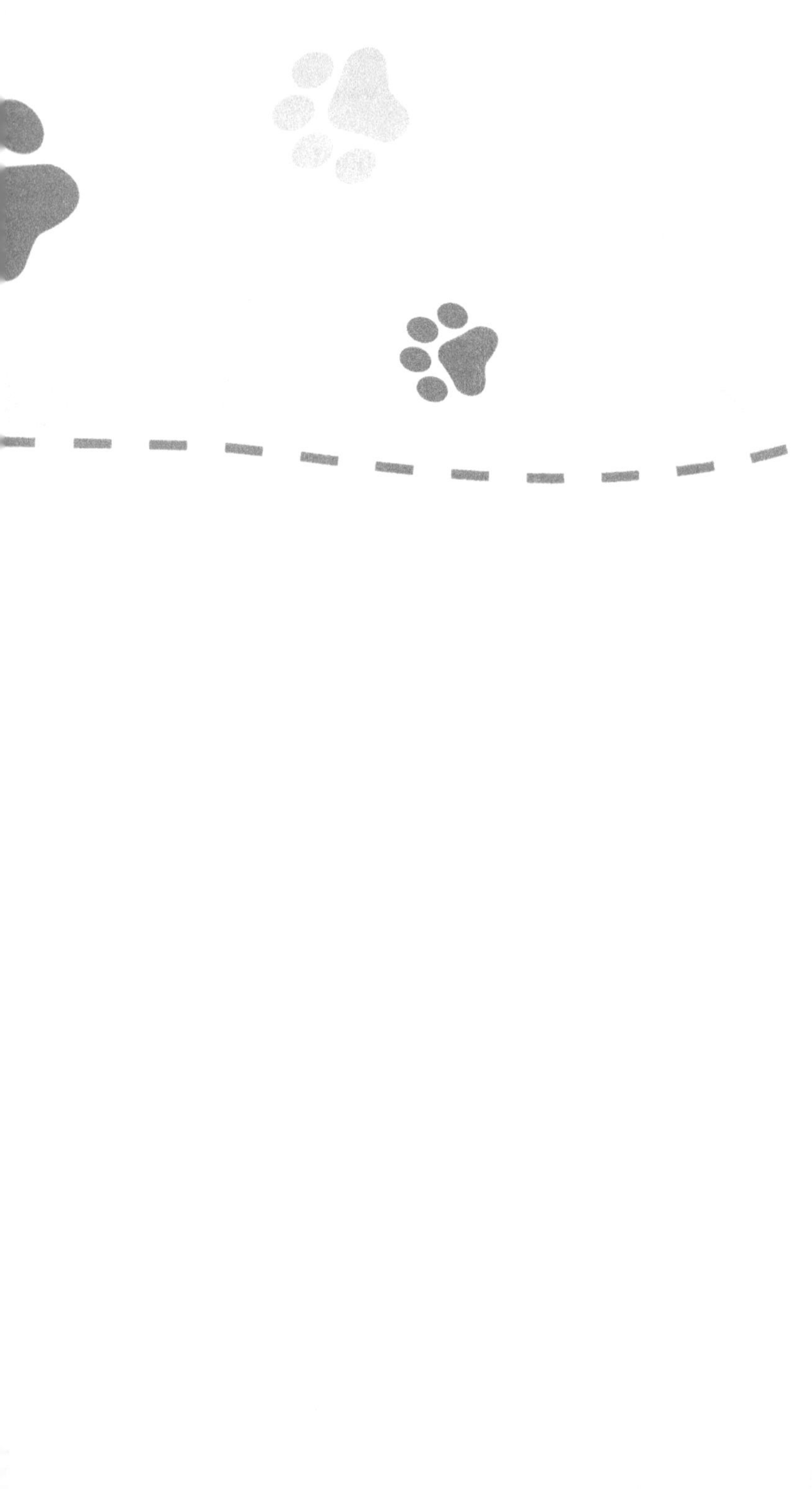

2

No one came running to investigate my violent break-in. Even though I waited by the door for a few long, uncomfortable moments, no one came at all.

Huh. Didn't expect that.

I shook my head, took a deep breath, and continued deeper into the dark building. First I checked the glass-enclosed conference room where the various members of the board got together to discuss important matters. No one was there, so I left the basket I'd prepared for my visit at the edge of the table and continued on to explore the rest of the building.

When I walked by Connie's office door, I couldn't suppress the shiver that ran down my spine. Even if she was there, I didn't want to disturb the vampire head of Commerce. Sure, she'd claimed she had no plans to eat me, but I felt better off not taking any chances.

I hurried down the long hall until at last I came to the vacant warehouse-like space where Mr. Fluffikins had taken me to kick off my last two assignments. This was the same place he'd flung deadly magic at me to test my instincts when I was temporarily appointed Town Witch. It was also where he'd entrusted me with the special silver brooch that had given me magic for my first assignment and served as surveillance equipment for my second.

"Hello?" I called hesitantly before inching my way into the room.

Only a weak echo of my own voice answered, so I dared to go deeper still.

Each time we'd entered this place before, Fluffikins had brought me to the center of the room and then jumped into the ceiling to retrieve that brooch. Might there be other magical goodies up there?

I decided to find out.

Now before you get all angry with me for snooping around uninvited, I'd like to remind you that this was the same agency that had already played fast and loose with my safety twice before. For whatever reason, they'd brought me on to help with their supernatural kerfuffle, and now I wanted to find out why.

Sure, the first time they brought me in, it was because I'd stumbled right into the middle of a crime scene. It made sense they'd keep me close by until things got sorted out.

But the second time they forced a job upon me? There was no obvious reason they needed me specifically. Not at first. But then Mr. Fluffikins accidentally dropped a few stray hints that there might be something special about me, something he and the others had yet to share.

For one thing, the boss cat couldn't undo the one spell I'd accidentally cast during my stint as Town Witch. He'd tried to turn my bubblegum pink hair back to its natural color but couldn't. Then after we transported to middle-of-nowhere Maine, he'd been about to tell me something before the investigation came crashing into us head-first.

I'd taken that all in stride and focused on the assignment, believing someone would surely explain everything once we saved the day and brought everyone home safely.

No such luck, however.

Not even a full three days passed between my first assignment and the second.

But now almost a week had passed since job number two, and nobody had bothered to get in touch. Not even Parker who lived mere feet away from me and used to drop by to visit unannounced.

So what was everyone hiding? And perhaps even more importantly, why were they hiding it?

I scanned the warehouse for an object that would be strong enough to support me but light enough for me to move on my own. *Nothing.*

Not one to be deterred, I headed back to the boardroom and grabbed a chair. This solution wouldn't allow me to look into the ceiling space with my own eyes, but if I stretched my arms high above and swept the area with my phone's camera and flashlight, I'd still be able to catch a glimpse.

Satisfied with this plan, I placed the wheeled executive chair beneath the missing ceiling panel in the center of the warehouse and climbed onto it slowly so as not to set it rolling. I probably would have been able to peek into the space myself if I stood on my tiptoes, but I did not trust my coordination enough to attempt that particular feat—

especially with no one around to help if I fell and gave myself a concussion.

So I reached one arm up, phone in hand and already recording, and held the other out to my side to help with balance.

As carefully as I could, I slowly rotated my wrist to make sure I scanned as much of the area as possible without having to turn the chair and myself around to face the other way, and then brought it back down to study the footage.

About ten seconds in, the glint of silver caught my eye. *My brooch!*

Before I could finish watching the full video, something heavy dropped from above, knocking me off the chair and onto the cold hard cement.

Ouch...

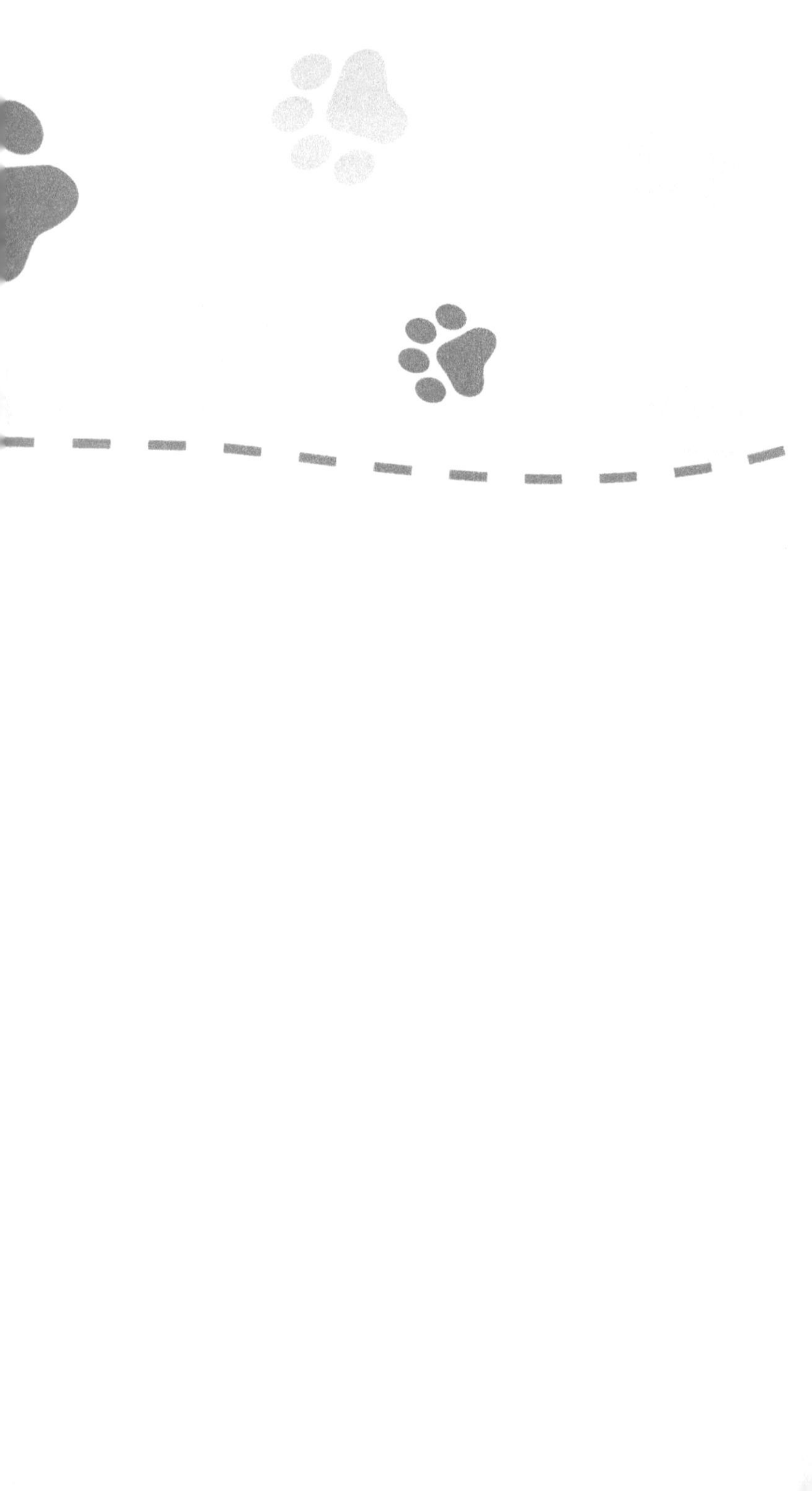

3

"ntruder!" Fluffikins hissed, staring down at me from the chair with judgment burning bright in his golden eyes.

"I'm sorry," I moaned as I tried to shift into a sitting position. Everything hurt so bad that I just stayed on the ground with my arms and legs akimbo. "No one had followed up about my next assignment this past week. And then no one was answering the door, so I—"

The cat shifted in the chair with a low growl. "So you thought you'd burgle us?"

"N-n-no," I sputtered. "I was just trying to find some answers, I swear!"

Mr. Fluffikins turned his nose up and let out an indignant huff. "You were just a temp, Tawny. *Were.*

Now it's time to let this go."

"I know I'm different." I wanted to sound serious, knowledgeable, and even a little intimidating. Instead, my words came out in a pained wheeze.

"I know I'm different," I repeated, sounding a little stronger on the second take. "And I know you know it, too."

The black cat flinched but gave no other indication that my words had made an impact. "I don't care what you think you know. You were not invited, and you shouldn't be here."

"Oh, I get it," I said, finally managing to roll onto my side with a grunt. "You only want me around when it benefits you."

Fluffikins chuckled dryly. "You really don't know much about how business works. Do you? Or cats for that matter."

"Whatever," I bit back. "You put my life on the line twice and didn't even pay me for it. The least you can do is tell me the truth about who I am."

The cat's tail flicked back and forth in irritation. "If you think you can goad me into saying something I don't want to say, then you're wrong."

Clearly, I couldn't appeal to the bureau-cat's compassion, so I'd have to bring out the final trick I had at my disposal. "I brought steak," I revealed with a scheming smile.

Fluffikins sniffed at the air. "What's that you say? Steak?"

"Yup, and it's no rump roast, either. I brought the good stuff." I paused to heighten the anticipation. "How do you feel about filet mignon?"

The black cat spun in an excited circle before hopping down to the ground and coming to my side. "Where is this steak, and why is it not in my belly yet?"

Leave it to a well-placed bribe to do what kindness would not. Inwardly, I breathed a giant sigh of relief. Outwardly, though, I kept my game face on.

"I'll get it for you," I offered, "if you agree to tell me what I want to know."

"Or I could beat you up and take it for myself." Fluffikins sneered at me as he weighed his options. "Come to think of it, you're already down and out. I just need to find that sweet, sweet steak myself." He sniffed at the air again, whiskers twitching as he trotted toward the edge of the room.

"Wait," I called before he could fully leave me behind. "It won't taste as good if it's ill-gotten gains."

The cat's mouth dropped open. "Is this true?"

I raised an eyebrow. "Do you really want to risk it?"

Mr. Fluffikins let out a massive sigh, then waved his paw at me. Instantly the pain from my fall disappeared just as fully as if it had never been there in the first place.

I pressed my palms into the floor, then pushed myself to my feet and waved for the boss cat to follow me back to the conference room where I'd left my carefully prepared parcel. Inside were seven Tupperware containers filled with freshly seared filet mignon. Yes, I'd gone all out, just in case I came across the full board in session and needed to bribe them all. Of course, I had no idea what Connie ate, given that she was a vampire. I also hadn't worried myself over bribing Melony since she was little better than a temp herself.

Having only Fluffikins to appease made this a very expensive bribe per capita, but I hadn't wanted to take any chances with what could very well be life-or-death information. Otherwise, why would he be working so hard to keep it a secret?

"First answers, then steak," I told the cat who was practically drooling as he sat across from me on top of the conference table.

"Steak, then answers," he countered, his voice

slurring even more than usual as he focused on the prize with wide eyes.

Well, I guess beggars couldn't be choosers. And in this case, I was definitely the beggar. I sighed. "Do you promise?"

"Yes, yes, and my promise is magically bound. Now make with the good stuff."

I nodded, opened the first container of steak, and slid it over to him. Luckily I'd already pre-chopped the piece, otherwise it would have taken much longer to sit there and watch him devour this medium rare cut into my last paycheck.

When Mr. Fluffikins finished, he licked his chops and lowered his eyelids with contentment.

"Well?" I said, when he made no move to keep up his end of the bargain. "Now it's your turn to make good on our deal. Tell me how I'm different."

"Ah yes. That," the cat said with a wink. "I promised to give you answers after steak, but I didn't say how soon I'd provide them. You'll just have to wait." He hopped off the table and trotted off down the hall, openly laughing at me the whole way.

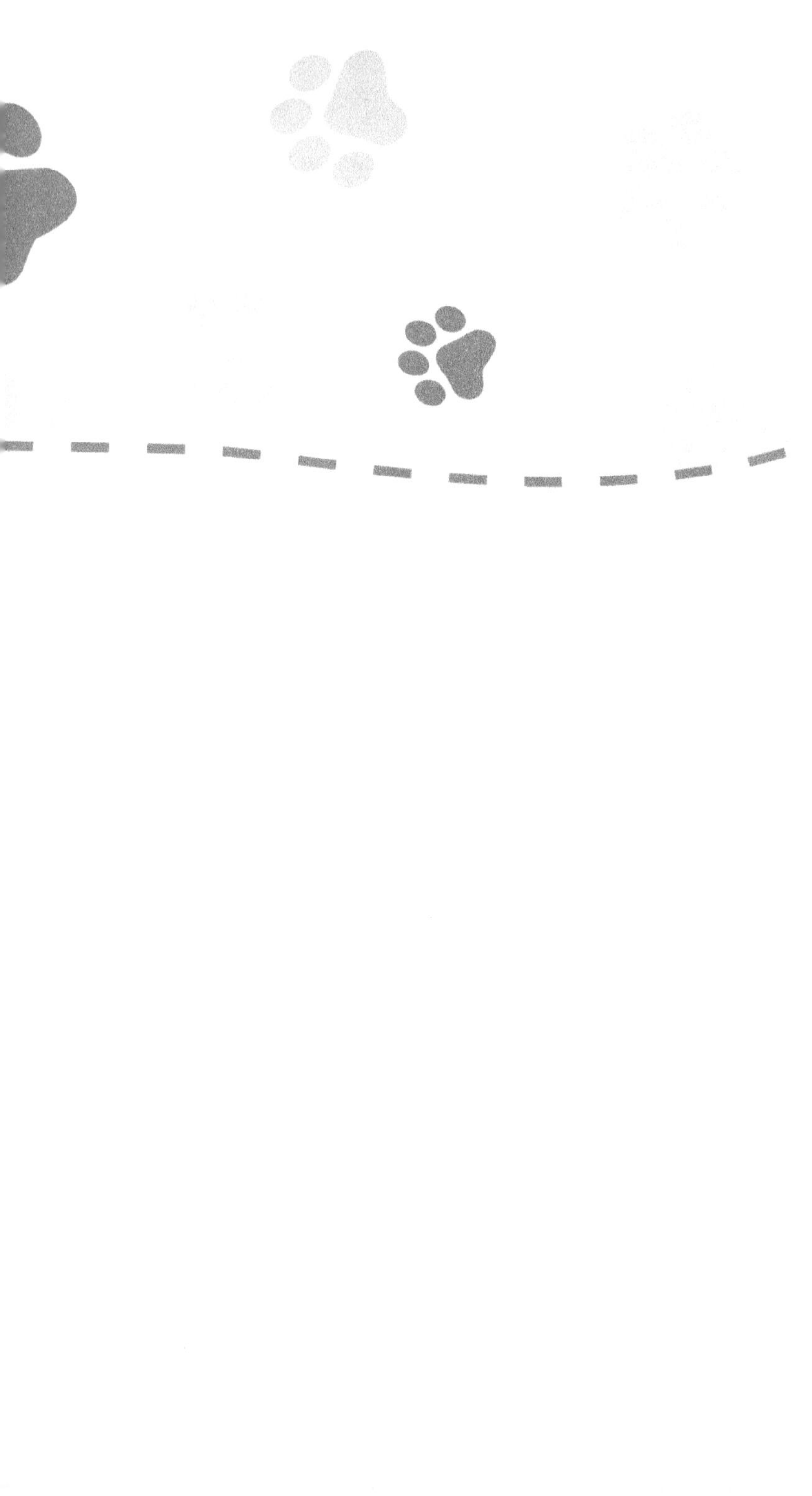

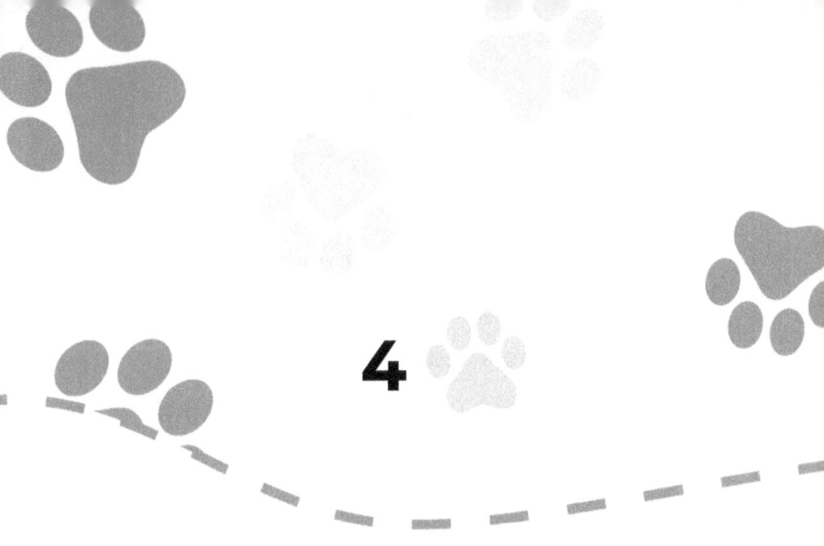

4

charged down the hall in pursuit of that no-good trickster cat. Once I caught him, I'd hold him down and force him to sign a contract. If I had to, I'd use the rest of the steak I'd prepared as leverage. I hoped it would work, because this was the only move I had left.

Now that I knew there was something special about me, how could I go the rest of my life without finding out what it was?

I caught up to Fluffikins in the building's abandoned front lobby. He stopped running and paused before the broken glass door. I had assumed he planned to yell at me about the destruction of PTA property, but he simply waved his paw and wedged the glass back together as if it had never been broken.

A moment later, the door opened and in walked Connie—the single board member I feared most. Today she wore a red crushed velvet shirt with an expensive-looking pencil skirt and designer heels. Her lips appeared impossibly pale when compared to her dark smoky eye.

"What is she doing?" the plump vampire asked with a stony expression. "I thought we'd decided to move on from this one."

Fluffikins let out a low angry rumble, almost as if he took offense to the way his colleague spoke of me. *Almost.* "Connie, you forget your oath. There is no discussing board business with outsiders."

"I have not forgotten mine," she answered with a sneer. "I am simply reminding you of yours. We've already broken protocol by including her in two separate jobs. So, why is she here yet again? Why hasn't her memory of us been erased?"

The two supernatural entities stared each other down, but neither budged in their position.

Maybe if I restated my case, Connie might be more willing to help than her boss had been. "I know I'm different. Not just a normie, I mean. And

I want to know why. The cat and I made a deal, but it doesn't seem like he's going to hold up his end of it."

Connie's eyes narrowed, and she shot a dirty look toward Mr. Fluffikins. "You made a deal with her?"

He shrugged his little kitty shoulders. "It had open-ended terms."

"Still, you made a deal with a normie. You know that's binding."

"She's not—" He stopped himself by hissing and unleashing a string of kitty curses.

"I want to know what you know," I said, standing firm in my resolve. I even thrust one hand on my hip in case that made me look tougher or more serious. Somehow.

"If you don't wipe her mind right now, I'll do it," Connie said with her jaw clenched. She looked so close to snapping, and I didn't want to be around when that happened. Still...

"But he promised me!" I cried, taking a giant step back as if it would do any good.

"You're lucky I have no desire to head the board, or you'd be out of a job," the vampire growled, curling her upper lip to show off those unsettling fangs of hers.

"Tell me and tell me right now," I demanded with a stomp of my foot.

"Let's make a provision to our agreement," Fluffikins shouted, his paw apparently having finally been forced—or so I assumed. "Steak for answers. Like you said."

"Now?" I had a hard time trusting him, given that last ruse of his.

The cat shook his head. "After one more job. With Connie." He turned toward the vampire head of Commerce. "I received your request for a temp to investigate the new coven downtown. Tawny will assist you in whatever way you need."

"Unacceptable." Connie's gaze turned even icier as she regarded us both.

"Actually," Mr. Fluffikins corrected. "It's perfectly acceptable, seeing as I'm in charge here. You need a temp, and this one's ready to take the job. Aren't you, Tawny?"

"If I do this, you'll tell me everything?" I asked, raising a suspicious eyebrow and crossing my arms over my chest like a shield.

He nodded, watching Connie instead of me. "After you've completed the job to the board's satisfaction, I will tell you what you want to know."

There was no way I was getting tricked by

another of his loopholes. "Define, *to the board's satisfaction.*"

The cat narrowed his eyes at me. "Until the coven either submits to Connie's leadership or leaves town," he answered with a small shake of his head.

"Deal," I said with a slight nod to show my agreement.

Connie cried and threw her hands up in the air. "This is not what I wanted when I filed that request, and you know that. I understand your desire to punish the normie, but why me? I've been nothing but—"

Fluffikins pushed off the ground with his back feet, then floated up to meet Connie's line of sight. He hovered in mid-air in a pink glittery swirl and said, "I don't care what you want. I make the decisions here, and this is what you got. As you know, I can't go back on a deal with a normie once made. You'll accept Tawny's help, or you'll forfeit your seat at the table. Do I make myself clear?"

Even though the boss cat wasn't speaking to me, I bobbed my head vigorously. Connie terrified me, but I could survive anything temporarily—and that's all this job would be. My last two assignments had been over in a couple days each. And I had to believe that this one would be no different. Otherwise I might run away screaming long before I got any of the answers I craved.

Be brave, Tawny. Be brave.

5

"Not so fast, Fluffikins," Connie hissed. "I know you think your word is law, but I refuse to work with someone I don't like simply because you used your stomach to make a decision instead of your brain."

"I have already made our promise. It is done," he said before floating back to the floor and landing with a soft thud.

"I have made no such promises to this mortal, so I will be the one to wipe her mind and free us all from the burden of her company." Connie grabbed my head and pulled it toward her. The rest of me followed.

"Please don't," I wheezed. I couldn't even struggle to get away. Connie's super-human strength controlled my muscles even better than I could.

"Look at me," she snarled.

And as much as I didn't want to, I couldn't resist the invitation. My eyes lifted from the floor and found Connie's waiting. They glowed a bright and hot pink, which normally made quite a lovely color, but as it lit the vampire's gaze, I froze in fear.

Literally.

I could not move. Could not blink. Could barely even think.

All I could do was watch as she raised a finger to each of my temples, pressed her manicured nails hard into my skin, and mumbled words in a language I couldn't understand.

And then just as quickly as she'd grabbed me, she let go and I fell to the floor. Thank goodness, Fluffikins had already cleaned up the broken glass or I'd be done for.

"Please," I mumbled, weak, tired, angry. "I only want to know the truth about who I am."

Connie gasped and looked as if she herself were about to faint. "She remembers? How is that possible?"

Fluffikins jumped up onto an empty desk. "I

cleared her mind once before. Barnes restored it after."

"But my magic is stronger than his!" Connie shouted and stamped her foot. "What is happening? Why isn't it working on her?"

"That's what I want to know," I added as I slowly rose to my feet. "This is the third time something like this has happened, and I just want to know why."

It was Fluffikins who spoke up next. "Our contract has been made. First tend to the new coven, then I will tell you both what I have discovered about our dear Tawny."

Connie folded her arms over her chest and turned her face away from both of us. "I will place a call for your removal," she promised the little black cat.

"And it will fail. Just as it has failed before," he responded without an ounce of emotion.

Connie huffed and pulled at her hair in distress, which seemed to please the boss cat. "I'll be in my office while she undergoes orientation," she said before storming off down the hall.

"Well, Tawny..." Fluffikins looked up at me with glowing golden eyes. "Are you ready to become a vampire?"

My breath caught in my throat. "Um, what? That wasn't part of the deal."

Fluffikins merely chuckled. "Actually it was. For your job with Connie, you will be provided with vampire magic."

"Fangs and all?" I recoiled at the thought. Even if Connie didn't suck blood, she was still cold, cruel, and downright villainous. I could probably survive working with her, but to become like her?

"Yes, you'll receive all the makings of the vampire. The power, the prestige..." He flicked his tail for several beats even though he clearly hadn't finished speaking yet. "The curse."

"The curse!" I exploded. "Nobody said anything about a curse."

"Come now. We should get you started. You'll have exactly forty-eight hours to complete your job, and there's no time to waste."

"What if I don't complete it in time?" I asked, chasing after him as he headed toward the warehouse.

Fluffikins turned to glance over his shoulder, his eyes twinkling with delight. "Then the change will be permanent."

That's when it hit me.

If I turned into a vampire for good, then he

wouldn't have to tell me why I was different. Because the answer would be obvious: *You're a vampire, Tawny.*

This was his last-ditch effort to keep his secret. He knew Connie wouldn't make my job easy. Heck, he was counting on it.

But I was counting on getting my answers. I'd survived two PTA assignments to date, and I'd survive this one as well.

My mortality depended on it.

I could've killed the sneaky bureau-cat. Instead I followed him back to the training room—ready to put everything on the line just so I could learn something about myself that I should have already known long ago.

If he wanted a vampire, then a vampire I would become.

I'd be the best vampire he ever saw, but only for forty-eight hours, tops. Then I'd be me again, and I'd finally know what all that entailed.

Game on, Mr. Fluffikins.

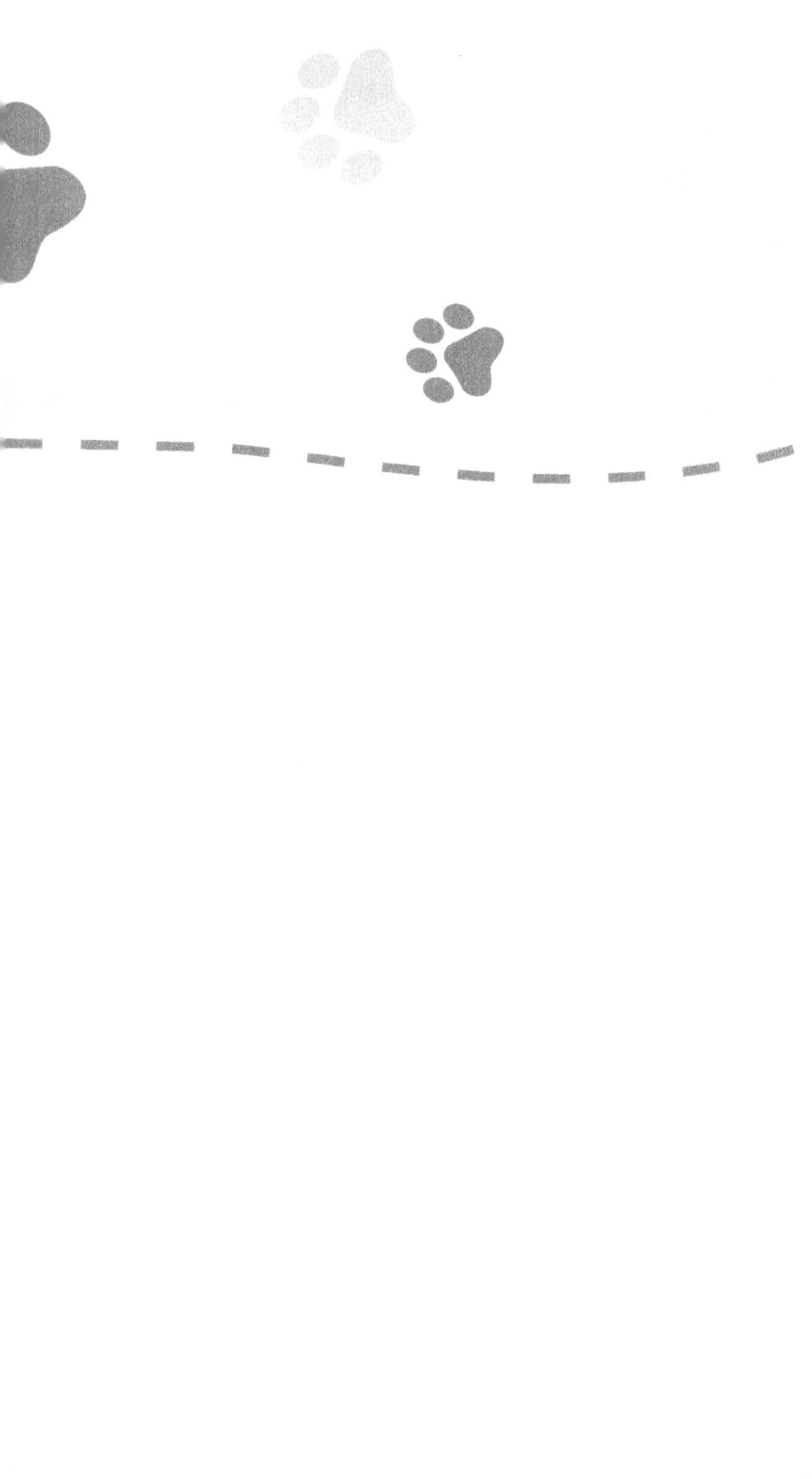

6

The warehouse was exactly as Fluffikins and I had left it only a short while ago. I pulled the chair I'd dragged in a couple feet away from the opening in the ceiling and took a seat. My body ached from my latest fall, thanks to Connie, but I doubted Fluffikins would have the good grace to heal me twice.

In fact, right now he was eyeing me with what appeared to be disappointment. "You look exhausted."

"I am exhausted," I snapped back. "And that's not a very nice thing to say to a woman... or to anyone for that matter."

A smile stretched between his whiskers. I wished he'd just get on with it already.

"You should be happy," he said dryly. "After all, you're getting exactly what you want. You came to steal the artifact, and now here I am about to offer it to you for your next assignment."

I slumped back farther in the chair and crossed my arms over my chest. "We both know this isn't what I wanted."

The cat's smile widened. I thought he might be planning to say something particularly mean-spirited, but he simply jumped into his ceiling hold, leaving me beneath him.

I expected him to return quickly as he had both of the other times he'd gone up there for me, but instead I found myself sitting alone for what felt like ages.

At one point, Connie even peeked her head in to check on our progress. She left, muttering something under her breath about "that no-good feline menace."

When Fluffikins finally returned, he held the magical brooch in his mouth, then turned and guided a second, larger object down from above with a sparkly swirl of pink magic.

"What's that?" I nodded toward the unexpected additional piece of equipment.

He gently lowered the brooch to the ground,

then looked back up at me. "It's your vampire armor," he answered matter-of-factly.

I cocked my head to the side. "Vampire armor? Like Greta's angel armor?"

"Not exactly. This will keep you from getting staked in the heart." Fluffikins sat and curled his tail in front of his feet.

My chest clenched at the fact that such a thing was even a possibility. "But I've never seen Connie wear anything like this," I pointed out, eyeing the ornate chest plate and the leather straps that presumably held it in place.

The cat scoffed. "Connie doesn't need to wear hers unless she's knowingly heading into a dangerous situation. She's a much more experienced vampire than you."

A shiver ran through me. "I'm not a vampire."

"Not yet, but you will be in about two minutes here."

"Okay, so do I need to wear this thing the entire time I'm on this assignment?" I took a deep breath in an attempt to ready myself. The thought of wielding vampire magic was far more terrifying than anything I'd experienced at the hands of the Paranormal Temp Agency so far. I mean, witches could be both good and bad, but weren't vampires always bad, horrible monsters? If Connie was any indication for how the rest of her species operated, then yes.

Fluffikins seemed to enjoy my discomfort and even took efforts to make it more pronounced. "I added the straps for you," he said with a small flick of his tail, "since you have a penchant for exposing the flesh on your chest, and we needed some way to secure it."

"You make it sound like I'm running around with my boobs hanging out. I only show a little bit of cleavage, and only sometimes. It's tasteful. Not wanton." Still, I pulled my top up higher and wondered if I should invest in some new turtlenecks for my wardrobe.

He looked me up and down and sighed. "Yes, well... The straps remain essential, nonetheless. We can't risk you dying mid-job."

"Aww, Fluffikins. I had no idea you cared." My voice came out syrupy and sweet. I hated that.

"Losing a temp mid-assignment creates too much paperwork," he deadpanned.

I groaned and rolled my eyes at the snarky cat.

He motioned with his paw to catch my attention. "Go ahead and put it on. I can use my magic to adjust the fit if it's not right."

I stood and hesitantly grabbed the floating vampire armor. It had a thick leather collar that buckled at the back of my neck along with straps that went under my arms and around my back to keep the chest plate from slipping. The metal piece was covered with intricately carved scroll work—an absolute stunner. Still, that didn't stop me from feeling as if I were wearing an oversized pet collar and that the boss cat may be trying to get one over on me rather than actually protecting me from getting staked in the heart.

The fit, however, was perfect.

I banged on my chest plate to show that it remained perfectly in place.

Fluffikins nodded. "Excellent. Now this." He nudged the brooch toward me with his paw. I wasn't sure where exactly I could put it, since the magical artifact was meant to stay close to my heart, and my heart was already covered with the breast plate. I ended up clipping it on my bra and hoping the metal wouldn't dig into the sensitive flesh below.

As soon as this artifact was in place, a glow lit me up from inside. At least that's how it felt. I don't think I was actually glowing.

What I do know is I felt very different.

We humans have become accustomed to a certain level of pain in our day-to-day lives, especially those of us nearing forty like myself. We have so many little aches and discomforts that become part of our norm—a rickety joint, an itchy patch of skin, that kind of thing.

The vampire magic took all of it away.

I no longer felt the pain from my earlier fall. I no longer felt anything. Not physically spent or in need of a second cup of coffee. Nothing.

I even held my breath for a moment and found that my lungs didn't yearn for oxygen.

Wow. It was as if I'd lost the sensation of living altogether.

"Well, how do you feel?" the cat asked, circling me now.

I didn't know how I felt about this change. On the one hand it was freeing, but on the other, it felt so at odds with my normal state that I no longer felt human. In that way, I guess I wasn't. I was a vampire. Did that mean I was technically the undead now? Yeah, it probably did. At least for a little while.

I ran my hands over my body and shook my head. "I feel... nothing."

"Oh, just you wait," Mr. Fluffikins added with a smirk.

"Huh?"

"Come with me. Now it's time for the real test of your magic."

I gulped hard, but it did nothing to quell my growing anxiety as I followed the boss-cat to whatever he had planned next.

Let's just hope it wasn't to my doom.

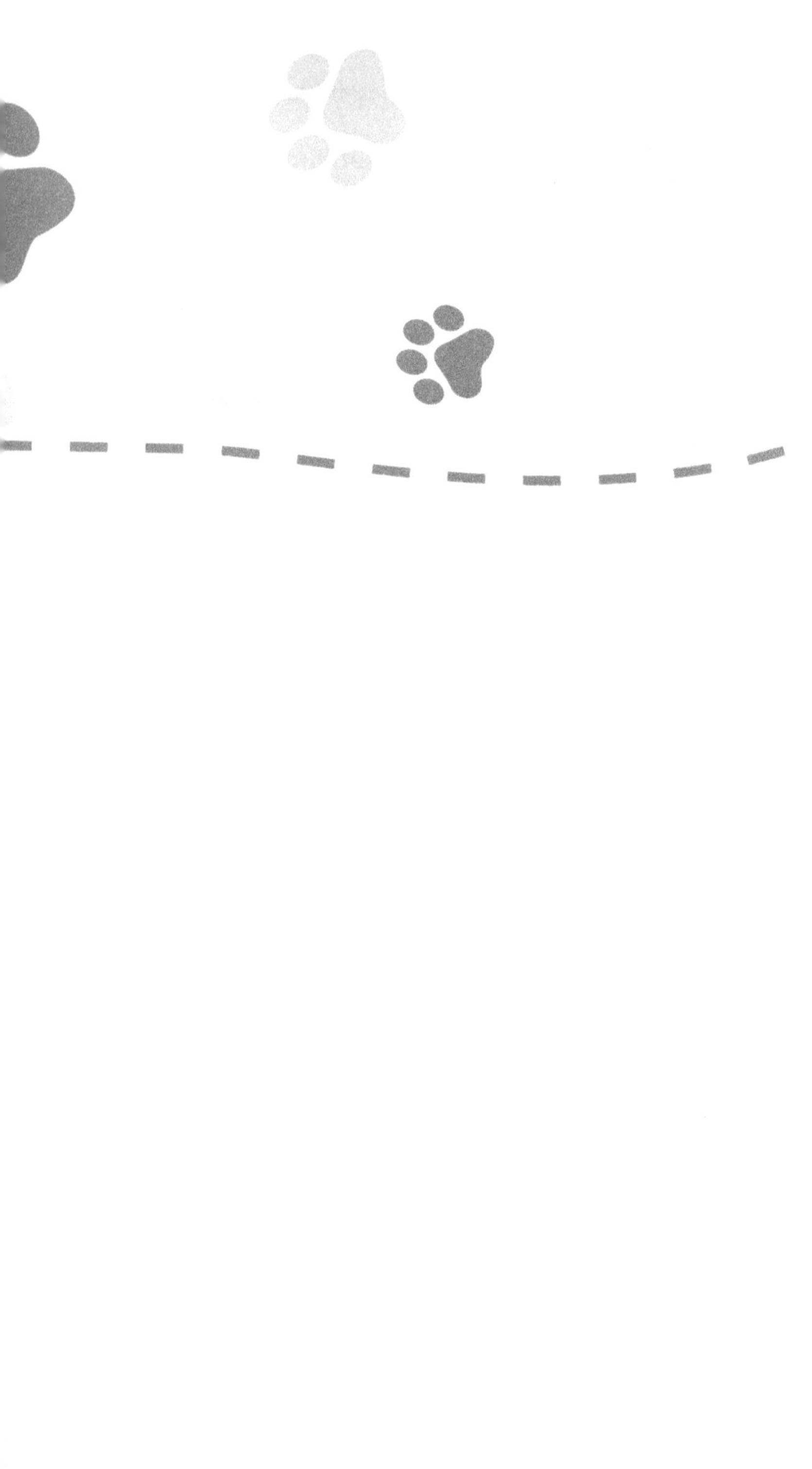

7

easily matched pace with Fluffikins as he ran full tilt through the office building's long halls.

This was so weird. At least when I'd had the town witch magic, I'd still felt like me.

Now, as a temporary vampire, I felt both elated and terrified. I could operate with extreme ease. Feeling no pain was a definite game changer.

But it made me wonder just how Fluffikins and Connie intended for me to put these new powers to use. Whatever the particulars of this assignment, I assumed they must be quite dangerous.

Instead of returning us to the conference room, Fluffikins took me to a small office in the back corner of the complex. "Wait here," he instructed, leaving me on my own.

I tiptoed inside and found what looked like an old-fashioned drawing room. The absence of windows and the presence of a busy floral-patterned wallpaper made the room feel much smaller than it otherwise should have. Hand-knitted doilies covered every surface, and a honey-wood curio cabinet proudly displayed a mismatched collection of dainty tea cups and saucers.

Unclear of how long my wait might be, I settled into a tall wingback chair, trying not to upset the doilies that rested over its thick arms.

The door swung open a moment later.

"Tawny? Hi." Parker offered a shy smile from the doorway. "What are you doing in my office?"

"Your office?" I crossed my legs, settling deeper into the chair. Still I felt no comfort from the plush, overstuffed seat. I felt nothing at all. "I had no idea this was your style."

Parker chuckled. "I haven't had a chance to redecorate since taking over the Town Witch post for Lilah. And part of me doesn't want to do it at all. It's nice, remembering her."

"You've been avoiding me," I told him. I'd tried so hard to get his attention this past week, but he'd definitely been avoiding me since our impromptu kiss at the end of my last assignment. I should have been overjoyed to see him now, to get the chance to talk. More than anything, though, I was curious about his sudden change of heart.

He sighed and leaned back against the closed door. "Since our kiss, I know. I'm sorry."

"Why?" I wanted to know. My foot twitched with impatience as if counting down the seconds to his answer.

Parker closed his eyes and tilted his head toward the ceiling. "I really like you, Tawny, but it's a lot to ask of someone, to accept all this PTA stuff. Plus, as you've seen firsthand, it's dangerous."

"I already know all that," I said, unwilling to let him off the hook.

"You know a little, but there's so much more, things that you shouldn't ever have to worry about. It's all my fault for dragging you in even this deep. I was selfish to bring back your memories. To kiss you." He winced as if the words caused him physical pain.

"Shouldn't I have a say in this, too?" I wondered aloud. I also wondered why he was being so dramatic. We'd kissed. Sure, it had felt momentous and earth-shattering at the time, but now? I didn't know how I felt. Mostly tired of having him run away from me, curious about why he had.

"We can't have a future," Parker revealed, concern reflecting in his gray eyes. "Magicks and normies, we don't mix for a reason."

There was only one logical conclusion here. We had to put this to the test. "Kiss me again," I said. "If you feel nothing for me, I'll let it go. But if there really is something special between us, shouldn't we at least see it through?"

Parker nodded and licked his lips as I rose from my chair and sauntered over to him. I placed a hand on his arm and brought my face to his— something I'd been longing to do all week.

And now that our big moment had arrived, I felt...

Nothing.

In fact, I'd felt nothing more than an amused curiosity from the moment he stepped into the office. Yes, we'd talked back and forth, and I'd made my argument for why we should be together. But that's all it was, a logical discussion. No pounding heart or shortness of breath as we drew close. No shivers of excitement from his kiss.

I'd crushed on him hard ever since we first met, but now he seemed little more than a stranger to me—one of billions on this planet. He could have been anyone.

Yes, I knew him, and I knew our history together. But that wasn't enough.

Parker pulled back and smiled at me, but when he caught the expression on my face, his brow furrowed with worry. "Tawny? What's wrong?"

I glanced down toward my new breast plate and shook my head.

"What's that? What are you wearing?" He raised a hand and brought it to rest on my armor.

"Mr. Fluffikins just gave me a new job," I whispered. "With Connie."

Parker's eyes lit with rage. He pushed me to the side and bolted out of the office without so much as a word of explanation.

I didn't try to stop him, but I did follow—curious more than invested in the outcome.

"You gave her vampire magic?" he shouted after storming into the conference room and finding the sleek black cat sitting across from Connie at the long table.

"Yes. Connie had a job," he answered with a shrug.

"But you know how dangerous it is! How sometimes the change isn't temporary!"

"And what's your point? We needed a temp, and she wanted another assignment. Remember, it's you who returned her memory after the first one. We could have all moved on with our lives by now if you hadn't interfered."

Connie smirked as she studied her freshly painted nails. I could still smell the sick chemical tang in the air.

"Are you ready to give us the rundown on the job?" I asked, stepping deeper into the room and moving toward Connie and Fluffikins to take my seat with them.

"Tawny..." Parker's voice cracked. I could see his anguish but felt none of it myself.

"Parker," I addressed him coolly, ready to move this along. "I have a job to do now, but we can talk more later. Okay?"

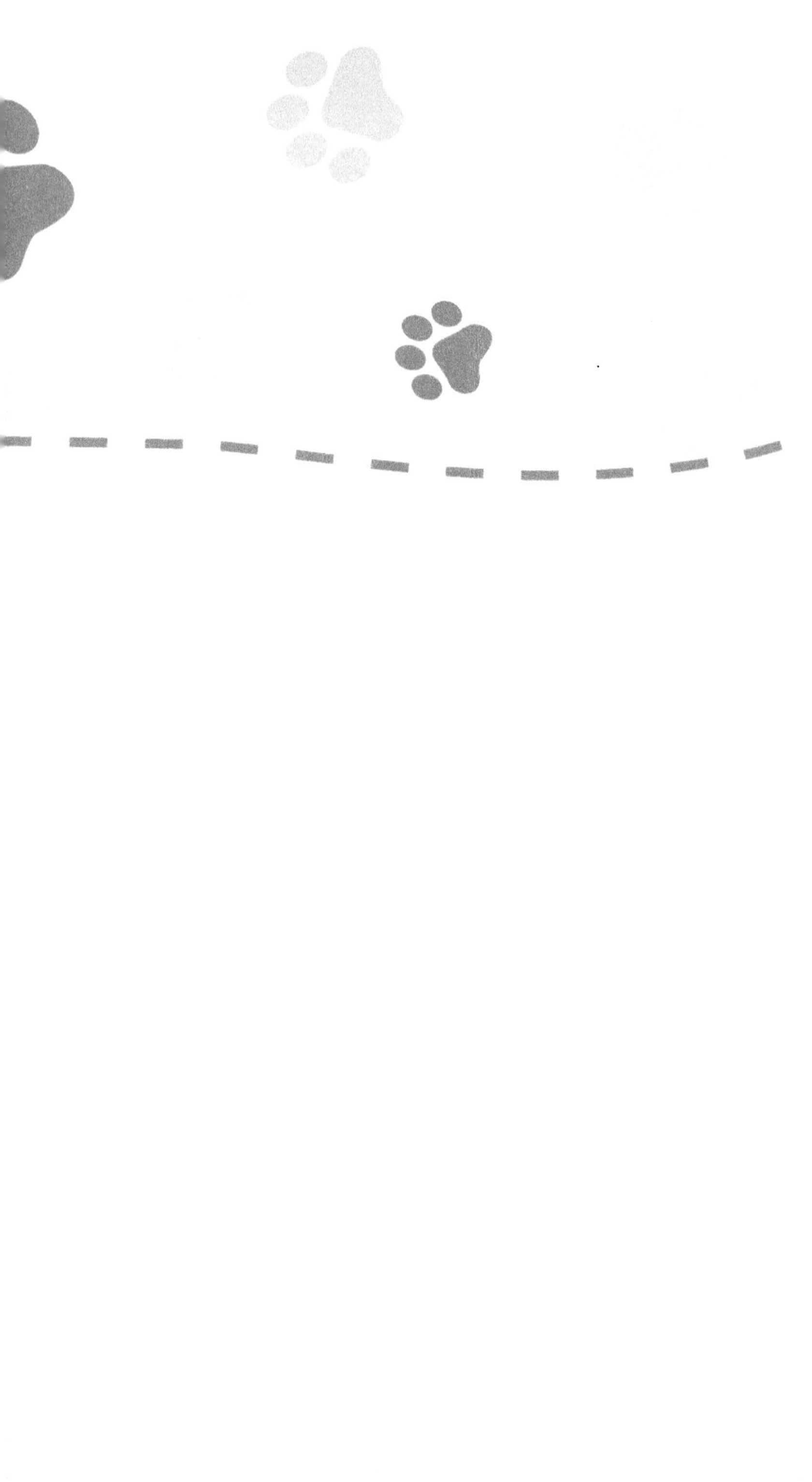

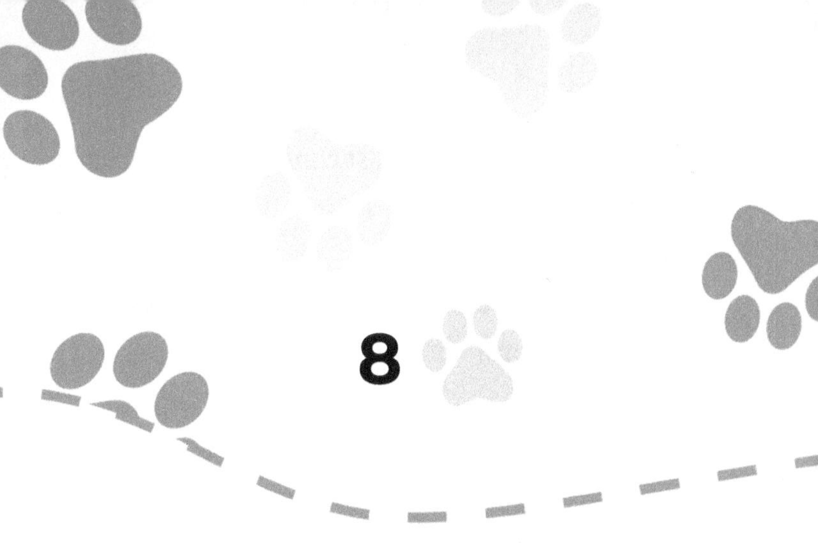

8

espite my request for him to leave and let us get down to business, Parker remained rooted to the spot. I had forty-eight hours, tops, to do this job, and here he was stubbornly delaying the start. If I failed this task, I'd remain a vampire forever—and he'd be at least partially to blame. How could he not see that?

"Have you told her about the curse?" he asked Mr. Fluffikins in a booming voice. I'd never seen him so riled up.

"I have temporary vampire magic," I informed Parker, pulling out a chair beside Connie and taking a seat. "That means everything that comes with it. And, yes, I know there's a curse."

"But do you know what it is?" he pushed even

harder. Why couldn't he just come out and say what he meant rather than asking all these senseless questions?

When I curled my lip instead of responding, Parker burst forth with his answer. "Vampires can't feel, Tawny."

Well, I already knew that. It was the first thing I'd realized when the new magic settled over me. And that stark absence became even more noticeable the longer I held onto the magic.

Parker appeared to be trembling now. His voice also quaked. "They can't love or keep any lasting relationships. Friends, family, romance. None of it. If you stay this way, you'll have immortality, but at what cost? You'll be a lonely monster forced to live by yourself in the shadows forever."

"Stop being so melodramatic," Connie spat. "I have the curse, and I get along just fine. Besides, she's not staying a vampire. I intend to finish this job and be rid of her as fast as I possibly can."

"So that's why you hate everyone," I quipped with a quick glance toward Connie.

She straightened in her seat and held her chin in the air. "No, the curse is why I don't like anyone. Hating them is a choice."

Fluffikins spoke next. "Barnes, your work here

is done. Thank you for helping me make sure Tawny's full magic is in effect before sending her out into the field."

"I want to help. Surely, whatever this assignment is, it will be done more satisfactorily with three people rather than just two."

"No, this is a vampire-only job. At least for now. See yourself out, witch," Connie commanded.

Parker looked as if he desperately wanted to say something to me, but instead he stalked off, slamming the door behind him.

"I thought he'd never leave," I said, which drew a laugh from Connie. I didn't want him to be upset, because it was such an unpleasant thing to witness. I needed everyone to keep their emotions in check so we could get down to business.

"Ha! I no longer hate you quite as much as the others," Connie mumbled. "I still can't wait to be rid of you, though."

That made sense. I nodded. "Mr. Fluffikins, are we ready to begin the debriefing?"

The cat rose to all fours and began to pace up and down the table in his classic war general stride. "The long vacant storefront at the corner of Main and Grand downtown has recently been purchased by one Vanessa Vane. A vampire."

"Just one vampire? That doesn't seem like much of a problem to me." I couldn't believe that all of this fuss was about a single vampire moving to town.

"Where one settles, there will be more," Connie said with a snarl, apparently having already made her mind up about this new resident.

Fluffikins strode back toward us, blinking slowly. "Before now, Connie was the only vampire in Beech Grove. Due to their long lives and extreme wealth, vampires are quite territorial. It's possible that Ms. Vane purchased property in town without realizing this area has already been claimed by Connie, but it's also possible she wishes to start a dispute. And if that's the case, the rest of her coven will be arriving soon."

"Okay, so what do you need us to do?" I asked, not quite understanding.

"As a lone vampire, Connie looks weak, but with your help, she'll appear more official. It means the newcomers will be less likely to make a play for the area."

"So what? We pay this new vampire a visit and nicely ask for her to leave?" This seemed far too simple, but both of my companions nodded emphatically in response.

"Exactly," they said.

I tapped my fingers on the table, growing impatient with them both. "And if that doesn't work?"

"Then you'll really get to see what those new powers of yours can do," Connie remarked with a sinister smile.

My curiosity sparked to life once more. I'd heard the expression about curiosity killing the cat many times before, but it seemed the saying was much more apt when it came to vampires. Rather than blood, I thirsted for knowledge, understanding. And presumably wealth, though I hadn't yet felt the avarice come to life within me.

Fluffikins purred with delight. "So are we all clear on the mission here?"

Yeah, about as clear as mud.

I bit my lip to keep from speaking. More out of self-preservation than any obligation to respect the boss cat. It looked like this job could go one of two ways. It could be the easiest one yet, or it could throw me straight into the middle of a violent vampire war...

And I honestly couldn't say which I preferred.

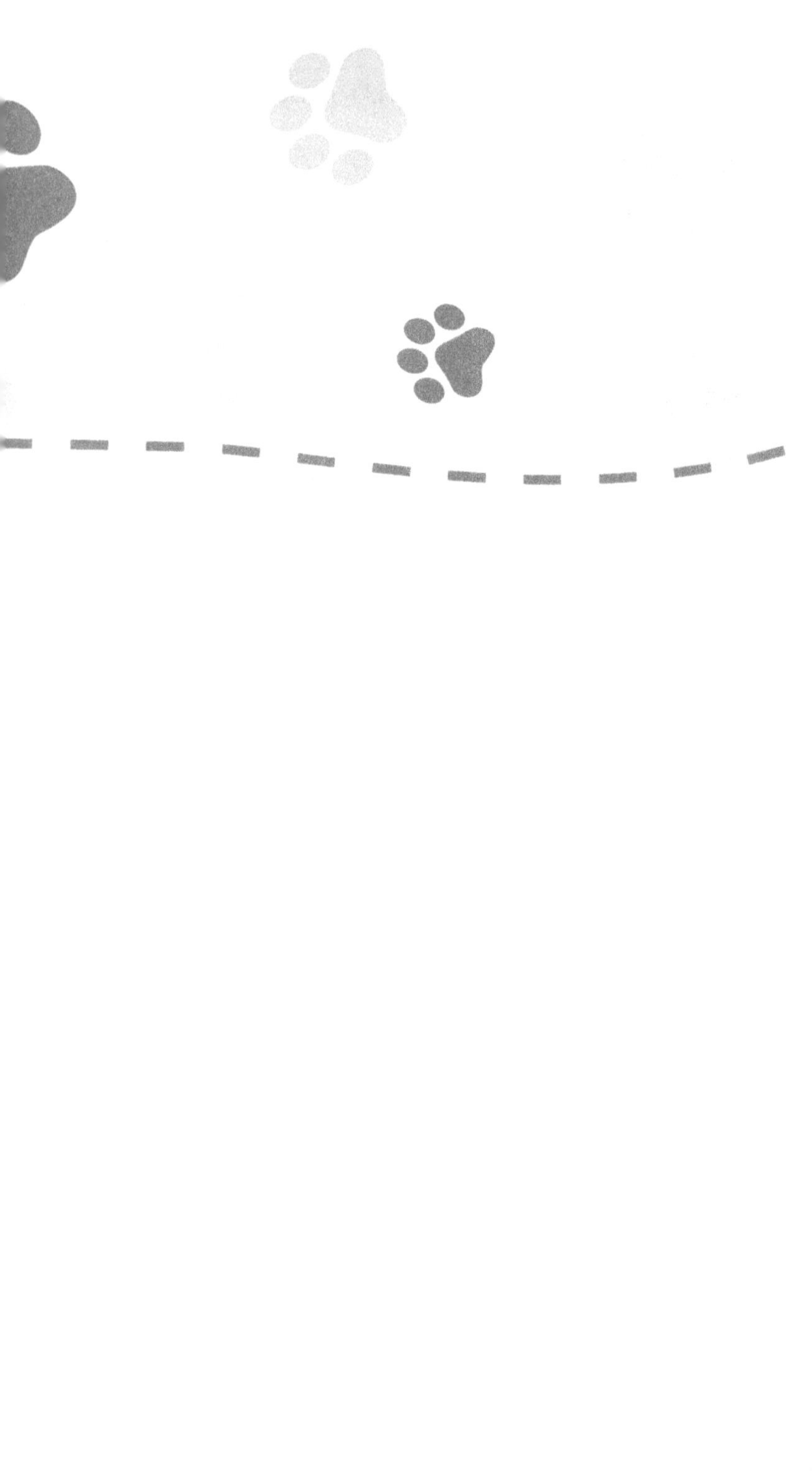

9

Fluffikins dismissed us from the board room, which meant it was time for Connie and me to find and confront this new vampire named Vanessa Vane.

"You look ridiculous," Connie informed me as we walked side-by-side down the hall. "Like you need to be attached to a leash and led around on all fours."

I brought a hand to my breast plate and ran my fingers over the scrolling metalwork. "Too much?" I asked.

"It's a fine accessory, I suppose, but it doesn't fit the outfit. A quick trip to my closet should have you looking like more of a respectable vampire, though."

I remembered Connie dressing me up as a phony psychic for my last assignment. That walk-in closet of hers went so far back, I couldn't see the end of it. Then again, Connie always looked like she'd stepped right out of a fashion magazine with her confident and put-together ensembles. I'd recognized a few designer pieces here and there, too, giving me no doubt everything she wore was painfully expensive.

Imagining the finery she'd put me in got me all twitchy with excitement now. Oh, so I could still feel some things. Vampires loved power and wealth, and according to Connie and Fluffikins, that was also how they now fed. Parker's kiss had meant nothing to me even though I knew it should have, but the prospect of playing dress-up had me all kinds of giddy.

What a strange new world I found myself in.

I tried to remind myself that this change was temporary. That I didn't have to guilt myself about not caring about Parker while I was equipped with vampire magic. But honestly, I much preferred focusing on the makeover ahead. How expensive an outfit would Connie put me in? I bet it would be more valuable than my entire wardrobe back home combined. I'd be so fancy, so deserving of admiration and respect. I could hardly wait!

Connie wasted no time in selecting a crushed red velvet blouse with bell sleeves and a pair of black pin-stripe pants from her closet and handing both to me. "If you're going to wear that ridiculous armor, we might as well make it work with your ensemble." She wrinkled her nose in distaste at my current attire.

"It's my vampire armor, to protect me from getting staked in the heart," I explained. Shouldn't she know this already?

She let out a sarcastic laugh. "Is that what Fluffikins told you?"

"Um, yeah. Are you saying he was lying? What does it—?"

"No time for questions. Get dressed, and let's go." She returned to the walk-in to give me some privacy and returned a few minutes later with a black leather corset in hand.

I eyed it—and her—skeptically.

"It completes the look," she said, helping me into it.

As Connie's hands wrapped around my waist to place the corset, I realized that we now wore the same crushed red velvet fabric. "Is there a reason we match?"

"No, not match," she corrected with a disgusted growl. "We coordinate."

"Fine." Working with her would be mentally exhausting. In fact, it already was. "Is there a reason we coordinate?"

She rolled her eyes. "Coven colors. Makes this little farce appear more official. Now, no more questions. With any luck, this Vanessa Vane will be a clueless coward and go running with her tail between her legs the moment we show up."

"Do you really think it will be that easy?" I asked as she yanked the straps on my corset as tight as they would go.

"No," she said, startling me with the abruptness of her response. "You've had two assignments with us now. Was either of them easy?"

"Fair point. Um, so how are we getting downtown?" I asked as she locked her office behind us.

"Well, we'll change into our bat forms and fly there, of course."

"Really?" I squeaked.

"No. Now stop asking stupid questions, and let's go." She moved quickly down the halls, but I had no trouble keeping up. We left the PTA headquarters, but instead of heading to the parking lot, we moved toward the woods.

As soon as we passed the tree line, Connie shifted into high gear. Together we moved through the forest so fast, it was as if we were flying. My new vampire magic removed all limits from what my body could do, it seemed. Not even wind resistance was an issue as we cut through the air and across the land.

In hardly any time at all, we reached the other side of the vast forest, and Connie slowed herself to an appropriate pace.

"That was amazing!" I cried, jumping into the air and pumping my fist.

"We move without restriction only when human eyes aren't near," she informed me, and for the first time I realized it took incredible effort to walk at this comparative snail's pace now that I knew how fast my magical body could move.

"What else can we do?" I asked, falling into step at her side.

"There is no we, and you'll do well to remember that."

"Vampires, I mean."

"You are not a vampire. You merely have one's magic."

I growled in frustration. "You know what I'm getting at. Just tell me."

Connie stopped walking and turned to face me with a stony expression. "I owe you nothing. If you have questions, find the answers for yourself. We're almost to Vanessa Vane's building. When we get there, I don't want to hear a peep out of you. In fact, it would be great not to hear any more peeps out of you before then. Just shut up, look tough, and let me handle everything."

Oh, was that all?

I was starting to think Connie would be an even worse boss than Mr. Fluffikins.

Less than forty-eight hours to go. I'd be counting down each one now...

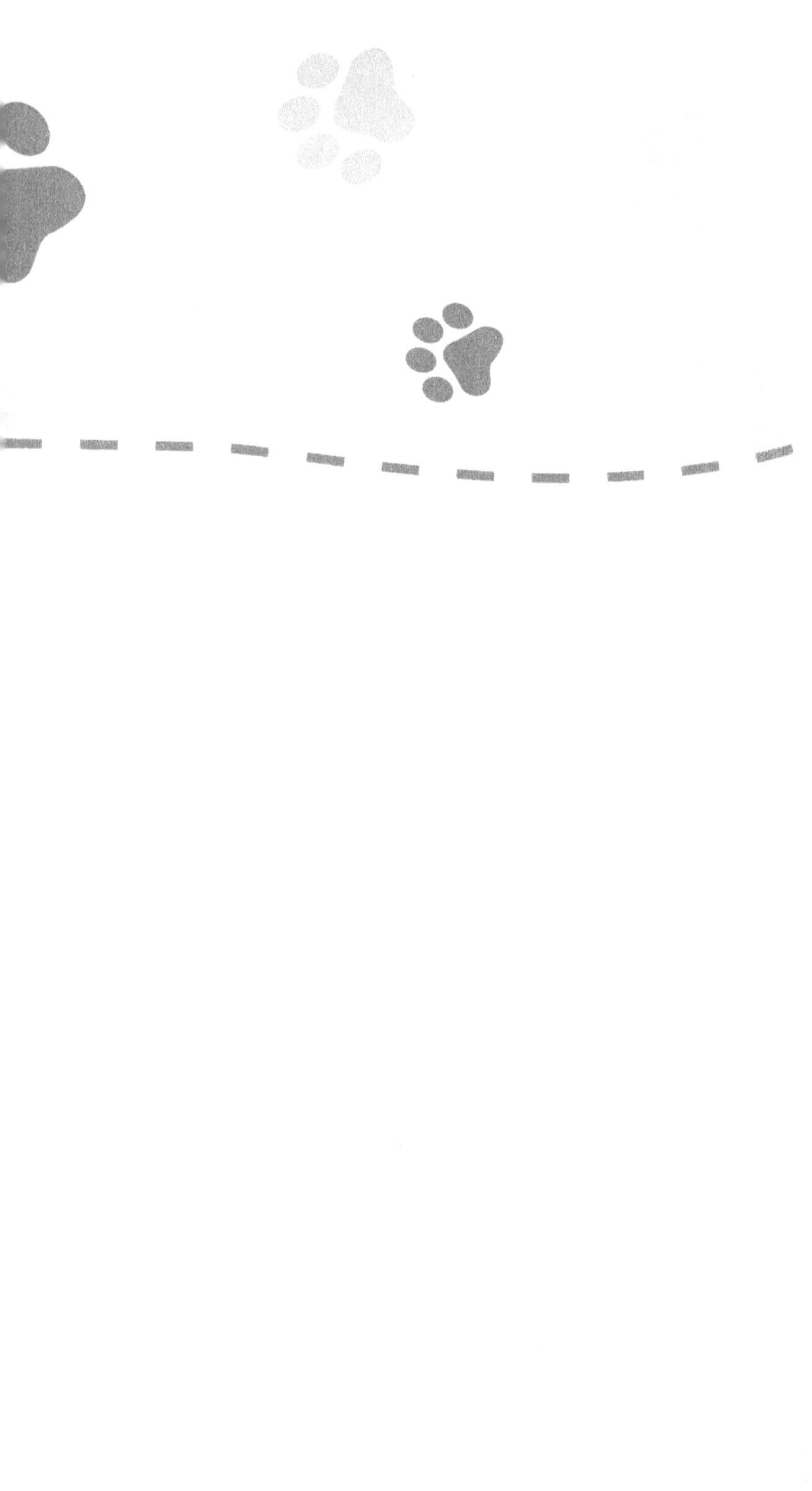

10

kept quiet to avoid any further arguments with Connie, counting down the minutes until this assignment would be over. Not only would I avoid staying a vampire forever, but I'd also find out the big secret Fluffikins wanted so desperately to hide from me. And I'd get another chance with Parker, which—logically—was something I knew I wanted, even though I couldn't bring myself to care in my current state.

What strange creatures vampires were. No wonder people feared them. If they only knew…

"We're here," Connie said, reaching out to clasp my wrist with her freshly manicured hand. We stood outside a storefront that had been bare ever since I arrived in town and likely a long time before that. When I saw it a week ago, it had been covered with cobwebs and layers of filth. Now the interior was decked out in bright, rich reds, yellows, and purples. Fantastic beaded mini chandeliers hung over each table, and a polished metal serving station stood at the back of the space.

"Is this a restaurant?" I asked in disbelief. "I thought vam—"

Connie shot me a look of warning.

"I mean, I thought people like you didn't have to eat." I glanced away from Connie and spotted the sleek sign that now hung above the shopfront: *BOLLYWEIRD.*

Connie saw it, too, and snorted. "We don't have to eat, but we can. Normally our heightened sense of taste makes the task more tedious than pleasurable. I suspect this get-up is for normie customers, though. Terrible name for a restaurant."

"I guess they're planning on serving Indian food. Not that it matters, if we're here to send them packing."

Connie tightened her hold on my wrist and waited for me to look her in the eyes. "Let's go. Don't forget your place."

Yes, I was the backup. There for no other purpose than to add to Connie's numbers.

I nodded, and she let go of my wrist. When I pulled the door open, she stepped in ahead of me.

A young woman stepped into the main dining area while drying her hands with a dish towel. She looked like she could hardly be more than twenty, but I knew very well that she could be centuries old, thanks to her vampire immortality.

"Can I help you?" she asked with a business-like smile. Her eyes narrowed when she caught sight of Connie, however.

Connie nodded in the direction from which the other woman had just come and quirked an eyebrow.

"Yes, we're alone," she said, crossing her arms and letting the dish towel dangle. "Now what do you want?"

This was obviously our good friend Vanessa Vane, and she also clearly knew who Connie was and why we'd come.

"As you can see, this town already has a coven in residence, so we'd like to ask you to leave and find another place to set up shop." Connie spoke in a chilling monotone, taking no efforts to hide her contempt.

"One vampire does not a coven make," Vanessa answered with an impatient cluck of her tongue.

"I'm a vampire, too!" I squeaked.

Both women shot daggers at me, and I nervously took a step back.

"What? Did you turn this one on your way over?" Vanessa asked with a cruel laugh. "Doesn't even have fangs yet."

"I've been in this town for a long time," Connie continued without answering Vanessa's question. "It's not big enough for the both of us, and you know that."

Suddenly, it felt very much like we were in an old western. I imagined the two vampires squaring off with cowboy hats and pistols. Never mind that we were currently standing in Bollyweird. This moment was all spaghetti western.

"I won't bother you, if you don't bother me," Vanessa supplied with a challenging glare. "Grand opening is tonight, and I refuse to miss my own event."

"We both know that's not true. It's not the way of our kind."

Vanessa sighed. *"Hmm.* Then maybe it should be."

I couldn't say I disagreed with her. Both Fluffikins and Connie had pressed the importance of getting Vanessa to leave town, but neither had told me why. What if Vanessa simply wanted to share her passion for south Asian cuisine with the rest of the world? Wasn't that a possibility? And if it was, did that mean we were the bad guys here?

I hung my head, wishing I'd asked more questions or at least been given more answers before marching in here to threaten a stranger.

"This is your last chance," Connie warned the other vampire through gritted teeth. "Leave."

Vanessa smirked. "Or what? You gonna make me?"

They continued to stare each other down, neither budging. Tension rippled through the room, growing thicker and thicker as the two vampires sized each other up.

I hung back, wondering what would happen next. Would we fight now, or…?

Connie let out an animalistic roar and spun toward the door. If this was the first battle, then we'd just lost. And that did not bode well for whatever happened next.

Connie swept back toward the door, grabbing my arm in the process. "C'mon, Tawny. We have a war to prepare for!"

Vanessa's amused laughter followed us to the

streets. She wasn't afraid. In fact, she clearly wanted this confrontation to escalate.

Which meant she was far better prepared than either me or Connie.

Which meant we had a pretty good chance of losing.

Crud.

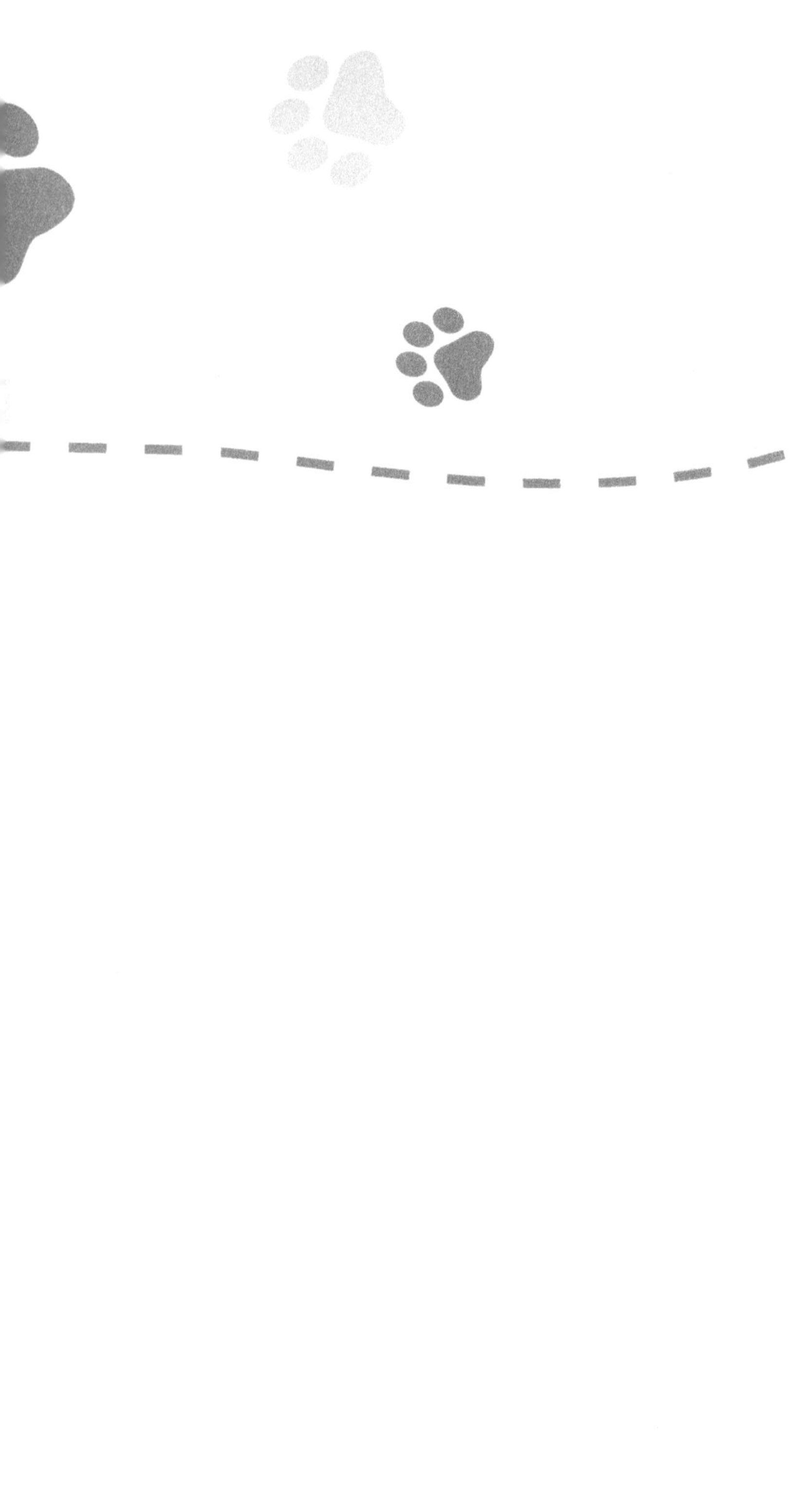

11

chased Connie through the streets of downtown. We both power-walked quickly enough to draw concerned glances from some of the other pedestrians, but I knew better than to mention it to Connie.

I waited until we were safely ensconced in the forest to unleash my long list of questions. "Why can't both you and Vanessa live here? Why is she refusing to go? Do we really need to declare a war?"

"Such pointless questions!" Connie hissed without slowing to discuss things with me.

"Tell me," I demanded. These were perfectly reasonable questions to ask in light of the situation and how very quickly it had escalated. "Why did—?"

Connie spun on me suddenly, and I nearly crashed into her. Luckily, I managed to catch myself just in time to avoid an embarrassing collision.

"When we first met..." the vampire said with a clenched jaw. Her muscles twitched as if she were trying very hard to hold herself back. "You were afraid of me. Why?"

Honestly, I was still afraid of her, but that was beside the point. "I thought you'd suck my blood," I answered meekly.

Connie eased up a little, straightening to her full height and looking down at me over her nose. "And what did I tell you?"

"That vampires don't do that anymore. They feed on wealth now." That was easy. Normally my memory wasn't the best, but when it came to the paranormal world, I now made sure that nothing I learned was forgotten. Even the smallest little factoid could mean the difference between seeing a job to completion or messing up so badly I lost my life in the process. I'd learned that the hard way when I'd forgotten what the various colors meant on the flashing crystal ball Fluffikins had saddled me with for my last assignment.

Connie's brows scrunched together as she regarded me. "That's not strictly true."

I gasped and stumbled back a step. "You still drink blood?" As a newly christened vampire, did that mean I, too, would soon be drinking blood? I shuddered at the thought.

Connie hung her head and eyed the leaves scattered across the forest floor as she spoke. "I don't, but I would if I have no other choice."

I chanced a step closer. "What would take away that choice?"

Her eyes snapped up to meet mine. "When too many vampires live within a confined area, and especially within more than one coven, there isn't enough wealth to go around. This leaves us to seek out other, baser ways of sating our hunger."

"Blood," I said, almost tasting the word as it left my mouth.

She bared her teeth, putting her fangs on full display. "We still have the equipment."

I ran my tongue along my upper teeth. They still felt the same as they had before Fluffikins provided me with my new vampire magic.

"You don't have them yet," Connie said, watching me closely. "But if the change remains permanent, you will. They only take a few months to grow in. It gives new recruits the chance to learn our new way of feeding and helps curb what would otherwise be a frenzy."

"Wow," I said and sucked a deep breath in, even though I know my lungs didn't need it. "So we really do need to get Vanessa to leave Beech Grove."

"Yes, and seeing my peaceful attempts at negotiation failed, we now must prepare for war." Connie's words came out dispassionate as she sighed and shook her head. She seemed tired, battle-weary before the war had even truly begun. Did she mean she was afraid? And if she was afraid, what did that mean for the rest of us?

"Have you been in a vampire war before?" I asked gently, hoping she may actually open up to me. "It sounds really scary."

She laughed dryly. "Vampire strength mixed with human weakness, what a joke."

"Have you?" I insisted. I'd seen that flash of despair, regret, fear, something—and I needed to know why.

"Many times. Where there is hunger, there is also greed. Some vampires aren't content with their current resources and seek to claim other towns. They must be stopped, swiftly and permanently."

"You mean...?" I took a deep breath and held it inside me.

The elder vampire reached down and grabbed a short branch from the forest floor, pointing it at my chest plate. "Stake to the heart. It's the only way to kill us, after all."

"You said *us*." My heart would have warmed if it had still been beating.

"I didn't mean *you*. I'm talking about the real vampires," she corrected with a growl. Oh, good. I'd offended her. That would make it easier for us to work nicely together.

"Then why did Fluffikins give me this armor to protect my heart?" I challenged, raising a hand to my chest.

She chuffed. "I don't know why he gave you that ridiculous collar, but it's not for the reasons he said."

"You think he lied to me?"

"I know he lied to you."

"But why? What's he hiding?" *And what aren't you telling me about your own past?*

"I don't know. I haven't been paying enough attention to catch on to the big secret you and he have been going on about. I also don't care enough to go digging."

Well, that made sense with everything I knew about Connie so far. She'd never liked me, and she never would. She couldn't. That was her curse, and for a short while, it was also mine.

She hurled the stick so hard I couldn't see where it eventually landed. Once the projectile flew out of sight, she looked over her shoulder at me and said, "Now can we please go back to base and start preparing for our battle? I'm going to need a lot more than you as backup."

Connie didn't wait for me to answer. Instead, she fled deeper into the woods, leaving me no choice but to run after her.

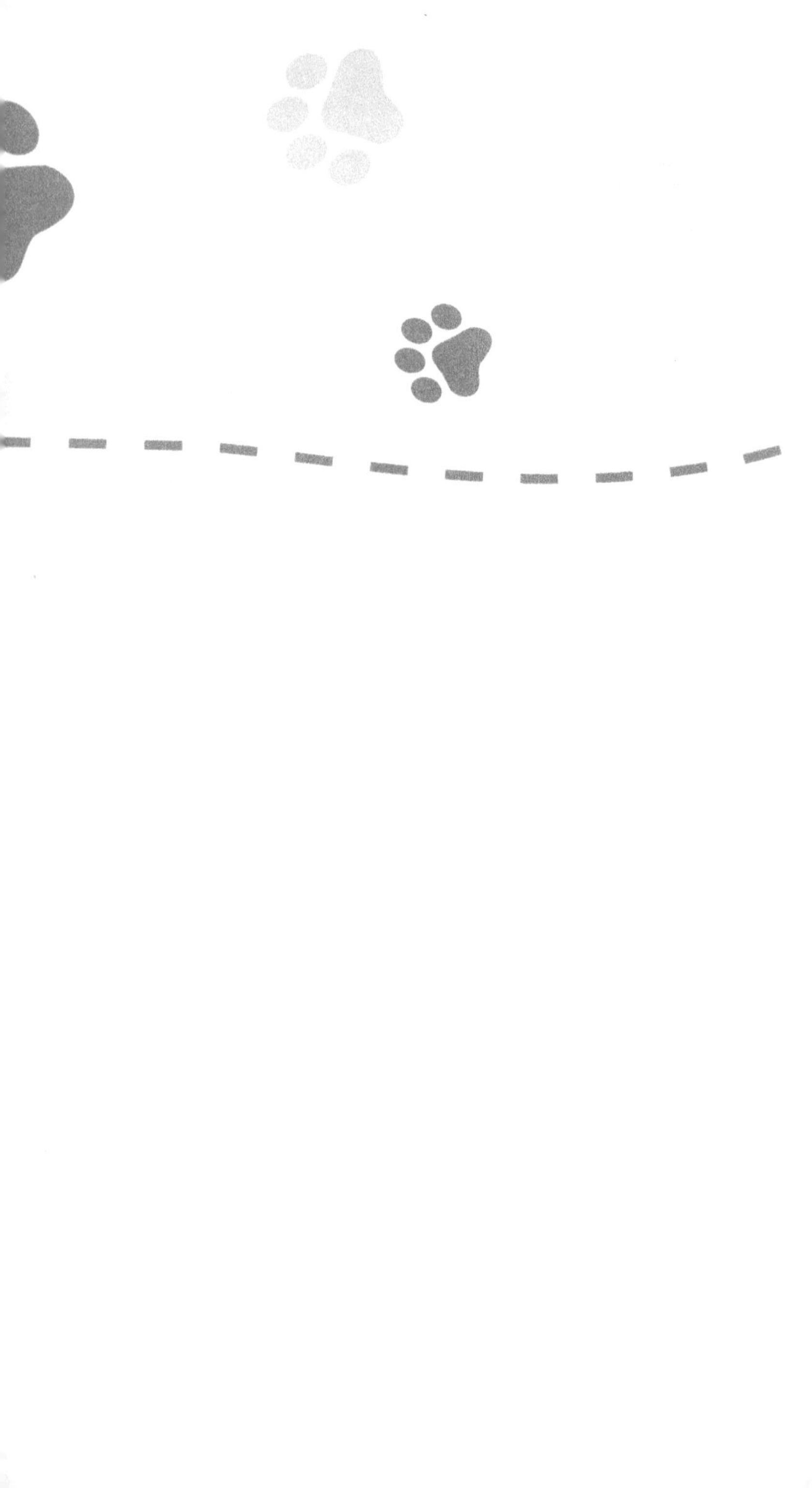

12

Mr. Fluffikins sat waiting for us at the edge of the forest. "Well, what's the report?" he asked as soon as we stepped out onto the lawn behind HQ.

"Time for phase two," Connie answered before setting her mouth in a firm line.

Fluffikins rose to his feet at once. "I'll gather the team."

"Leave the angel out of it," Connie snarled, her expression growing dark in an instant. "She's never liked my methods, and she doesn't hesitate to say so, either. If we're going to create a strong team, we need no dissidents."

The cat nodded. "Very well."

"What now?" I asked Connie as Mr. Fluffikins trotted back toward HQ.

She stared after him rather than shifting her gaze to meet mine. "Now we form a plan and practice until I'm reasonably assured you won't fail."

"How to fight a vampire one-oh-one?"

She smirked. "Something like that."

Fluffikins worked fast, so it wasn't long before the others joined us at the edge of the forest.

Parker immediately rushed over to stand at my side. "Tawny, are you okay? What's going on?"

I shrugged and shook my head. I didn't fully know the answer to either of his questions.

"All eyes on me, please," Connie shouted at us. "You're here to learn how to dispatch an unwanted coven in the area. I'll formulate a plan and then teach each of you how to execute it."

The old guy in the suit lowered himself to the forest floor, struggling for breath. If his waist-length white beard hadn't given away his age, then his complete lack of physical fitness would have sold him out. I still didn't know his name, and at this point, it felt rude to ask. I did know that he was the head of Cemeteries, which was the most cringey job of the bunch. Seriously, though, what good would such a feeble old man be when it came to violent hand-to-hand combat?

Connie cleared her throat to draw everyone's attention back to her and continued. "Clearly, we are at a disadvantage here with our hodgepodge group of supernaturals, a normie with magic she doesn't know how to use, and a teenager."

"Hey!" Melony and I cried in unison.

"I'd know how to use my magic if you'd just teach me," I shouted at Connie.

"And I'm eighteen. That makes me an adult!" Melony protested.

"If you say so," I muttered loud enough for her to hear.

"At least I come from a line of powerful magicks!" she shot back.

"At least I save lives instead of trying to take them!"

"Well, at least I—"

"Enough!" Connie yelled so loudly her reprimand shook the trees.

Melony and I immediately stopped our bickering and crossed our arms over our chests. Again in perfect unison.

If you thought that my saving her life last week would have turned her to my side, then you'd be wrong. She was still bent out of shape about our first encounter a few days before that—the one where she and her grandpa tried to kill me, but I survived and managed to help foil their evil plans. It didn't matter that I'd gone all the way to Maine to free her from some weird magical hostage situation. She still hated my guts. The brat.

"Vampires are stronger, faster, and smarter than all of you put together. They're also much harder to kill," Connie continued.

"Wait, why isn't Greta here?" Buckley, our head of Agriculture, asked.

"You know how I feel about the angel," Connie answered stonily.

Tension rolled off Connie in thick, angry waves, and we all averted our eyes to keep from upsetting her further.

"So as I was saying, under normal circumstances, none of you stand a chance against a vampire. That's why we have to make sure the circumstances aren't normal." She paused to let that sink in.

"The temp and I went downtown to meet Vanessa Vane this morning, and she mentioned her restaurant would be opening tonight. If there are more in her coven, I have no doubt they'll turn up for the event. What we don't know is how many outsider vampires we're actually dealing with. We can't know, which makes it that much more important to be prepared for anything."

Mr. Fluffikins, who had been uncharacteristically quiet up until the point, hopped onto a low tree branch to address the group. "For this assignment, Connie is lead. I expect you to give her the full measure of respect you'd normally give me."

I began to snicker under my breath but quickly covered it with a cough. "Sorry," I mumbled, bringing a hand in front of my mouth to hide the smile that lingered.

"We'll go in tonight during the opening." Connie kept her threatening gaze on me while she addressed the full group. "I'll need half of you inside and half on the streets."

Parker raised his hand. "Tawny and I can go inside. Make it look like a date."

"Perfect," Connie agreed, a slow smile curling on her lips. "Melony, you can team up with Buckley to do the same."

"But he's like the same age as my dad!" the eighteen-year-old witch protested.

Buckley tossed her a wink, which drew laughs from me, Parker, and the old dude in the suit.

"I promise to be the perfect gentleman," Buckley said, rolling up the sleeves on his ubiquitous plaid shirt as if he were ready to get down to business right now. "Although I'll probably need to change into something more suitable."

"Exactly what I was thinking," Connie said.

"Will I need to wear something fancy, too?" I asked, unsure whether my vampire get-up fit the bill for a small-town restaurant opening.

"She's not talking about clothes." Buckley gave me a bright smile, and then with a poof, he disappeared right before my eyes.

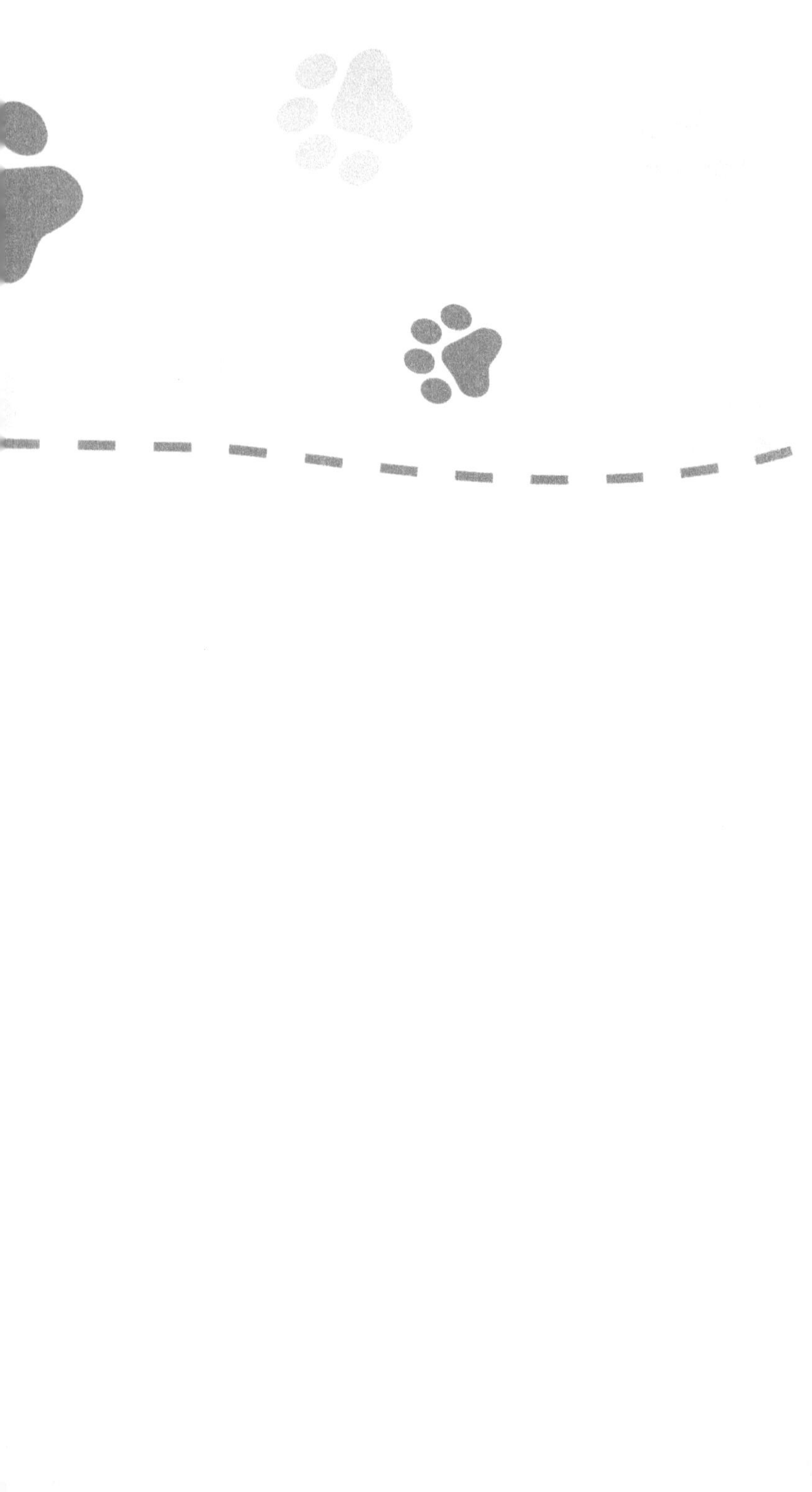

13

A little sparrow appeared as if out of thin air and flew over to perch next to Mr. Fluffikins on his tree branch.

"Whoa, what just happened? Where's Buckley?" I cried, spinning around to search for him.

"Relax, I'm right here," the little bird chirped. "Didn't you know that I'm a shifter?"

"That's why he oversees Agriculture," Parker explained from beside me. "It's easy for him to get a lay of the land because he can turn himself into any animal he wants, so long as its native to this area."

I stared at the sparrow, my jaw hanging open in astonishment. "Why the restriction? Can't magic do anything?"

"Magic isn't meant to be flamboyant and attention-catching. It can only exist if safely hidden," Parker explained.

"Enough," the vampire in charge bellowed. "This isn't meant to be a lesson on shifters for our one normie. This is about vampires and making a plan to stop them. Buckley, go scope out the building. It's that new Indian restaurant at the corner of Main and Grand. Try to get a sense of how many vampires we're dealing with here. Don't return until you have gained information we can use."

The bird nodded its cute little head and then flitted away. I soon lost sight of it amidst the tall dark trees.

"You're a vampire, Connie," Parker said with a playful grin. "So, then tell us, how do we kill you?"

Connie bared her fangs and fixed a predatory gaze on Parker.

"Rules for the undead are different," the old guy in the suit said. "Otherwise, I'd give 'em a whoosh and a whoop." He mimed swinging something— maybe a baseball bat—then whooped again.

Parker nudged me in the arm with an explanation for that, too. "He's our reaper."

A reaper, oh!

I stood on tiptoe to whisper into Parker's ear. "What's his name?"

Parker shrugged. "That's the thing. No one knows. I don't even think he does."

"How could he not know his own name?" I asked, perhaps a little too loudly.

"Call me R," the old guy shot in. "And thank you for asking... even if you didn't ask me."

"How do you not—?"

"All side conversations must cease!" Connie bellowed, sending another vibration through the forest.

The next thing I knew she stood behind me with an arm drawn across my neck in a tight hold. "Vampires are fast," she said, then nipped at the air beside my ear. "They can kill you just as soon as look at you."

Connie let me go and popped up behind Melony, putting her in the same chokehold. "So what do you do?"

Melony writhed and struggled in Connie's arms but failed to break free.

Connie laughed. "Vampires are strong, too. Think you can spar with one and come out the victor? Think again, princess."

She released Melony, and the young witch fell to the ground in a heap.

Next Connie came for Parker, but instead of taking him in her hold, she wound up face down on the forest floor. It all happened so fast, I had no idea how he'd bested her.

"Very good," Connie said, popping back to her feet and dusting herself off. "Now tell the others how you did that."

"Never lose sight of the target."

Connie nodded. "Good. What else?"

"Use their speed against them. Fast movements can lead to powerful falls."

Connie zoomed up behind R. He took a step to the side, and Connie flew past him, moving too fast to change course at the last fraction of a second.

"Evasive tactics work," Connie announced with a tight smile. "Until they don't."

She flew at R again, but he sidestepped her once more. She kept doubling back and hurling herself at him until she at last managed to tackle him.

"See," she said with a huff. "Evasion is a stall tactic, not a winning one."

"Oh, I could have gone all day," R revealed with a wink. "But I figured the sooner you made your point, the sooner we could all get on with our day." The old guy could certainly move fast when he wanted to. I was beginning to think our reaper in residence was much more than he seemed at first glance.

Connie growled in frustration, then launched herself at me. She moved fast, but now so did I. I threw my arm back, making a fist.

It connected with my target.

"Ouch!" Connie shouted, even though I knew she couldn't feel the pain. Maybe she was so used to having to pass as human, it had become an automatic reaction. Or maybe her pride had been wounded so badly, she couldn't help crying out.

She turned around and came rushing back. This time, she managed to overtake me.

"The moment you become overconfident is the moment you lose," she warned with a haughty look of satisfaction.

She let me go but continued to throw herself at us, one at a time.

Again and again.

And again.

I'd never been an exercise person, but this training activity was fairly easy now that I knew what to do. The vampire magic came with perfect physical fitness. I couldn't grow tired, get injured, or slow down.

But neither could Connie.

Nor could our enemies.

While helpful, I doubted this afternoon of training would actually be enough to prepare us for victory.

Oh, how I hoped I was wrong about that.

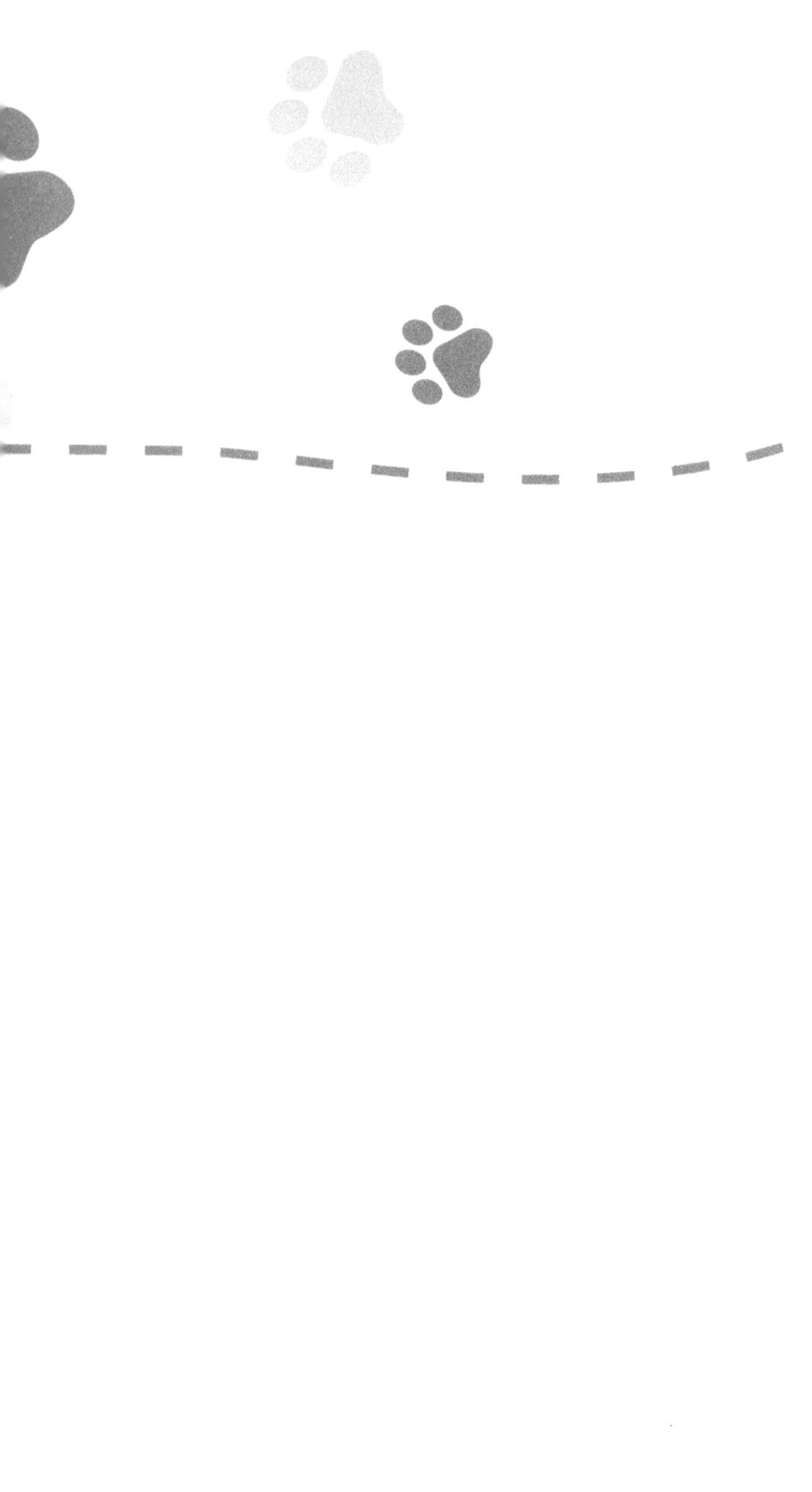

14

Connie's training went on for so long that the non-vampires among us showed notable signs of fatigue. Their success rate for besting Connie had already spiked and was now on a clear and rapid decline. Which made me wonder if, by this point, it was even helping at all.

"Um, maybe we should all take some time to recharge before tonight's operation," I suggested as Connie clutched Melony against her chest.

"Vampires don't need rest!" Connie spat back.

"But people and witches do," Parker pointed out.

I glanced toward R with burning curiosity.

He just smiled and shrugged. "Reapers aren't

like vampires or humans, or really anything or anyone else. Don't worry about me. I'll manage."

"I'm worried about all of you," Connie grumbled. "Our chances aren't good, especially if we're dealing with a full coven."

A rustling of leaves sounded from deeper in the forest. Connie and I both turned toward the sound, but the others didn't seem to hear anything until the rustling drew closer.

A tall, tan buck with a massive rack of antlers ran straight for us, his hooves beating hard against the earth as he approached.

"Buckley, report," Fluffikins called from the spot where he'd been napping in his tree for much of the day. I hadn't realized that he'd woken up until he spoke.

When I shifted my eyes from the cat back to the deer, I found the buck had gone and left Buckley standing in his place.

Oh, now I got it.

Buck. Buckley. Ha.

Thankfully, his shifting magic returned him in a fully dressed state. I don't think I could have handled getting so intimately acquainted with him —or anyone else—in the midst of all of this.

In addition to his flannel shirt and jeans,

however, Buckley also wore a frown. And that concerned me.

"Speak," Connie prompted when Buckley hesitated for too long.

"It's n-not good," he sputtered at last. "I counted at least four more vampires joining the first."

"Will there be more?" Connie demanded. "Did you hear anything of their plans?"

"That all remains unclear. Regardless, we should act fast to minimize risk."

Fluffikins jumped down from the tree branch and paced our way. "Agreed," he said, walking past our group and heading for the edge of the woods.

"What time do they open tonight?" Connie asked.

"Seven," Buckley answered, eager to show he had at least brought some answers back with him.

"Then we'll plan to be there at seven thirty. Our four inside men are dismissed. R, join me and Fluffikins at HQ, so we can plan our movements on the outside."

Melony crossed her arms and kicked at the ground. "Um, men? It's the twenty-first century, lady vampire. Perhaps you could try being a bit more gender inclusive?"

"Oh, did I hurt your little mortal feelings?"

Connie mocked, her eyebrows arching high. "Try living for several centuries, then tell me how important current social niceties seem to you. Now like I said, dismissed. Don't make me tell you a third time."

"Or what?" Melony challenged, flinging a defiant hand on her hip.

"Okay, that's enough. C'mon, Melony." I wrapped an arm over her shoulders and forced her to exit the forest with me.

"Let go of me!" she roared, but she was unable to escape my strong grasp, thanks to my vampire magic. I was just as strong and fast as Connie, although still unpracticed.

I would be okay tonight, but what about Melony? Parker? The others?

The witches seemed so vulnerable. Even Buckley would be at a disadvantage as a shifter. So far I'd only seen him transform into a sparrow and a deer. Parker had said he could only turn himself into local animals, and I doubted he'd get far as a wolf or a gator in the middle of a packed restaurant or busy street.

I still didn't fully understand what Fluffikins could do, even though I knew he was a powerful magic user. Good offense didn't necessarily translate to a superior defense, though. For all I knew, he could be the most at risk of us all.

Which meant it was that much more important that Connie and I take lead on this.

The two of us against at least five vampires who presumably already knew how to work well together and had had much more time to come up with a plan. Those weren't good odds.

But if the PTA didn't succeed, everyone in town would be at risk. I didn't know how often vampires needed to feed, but I doubted anyone in Beech Grove would want to lose their lives to a late-night predator.

If they took even one person, it would be too much.

We had to win.

Or die trying.

It felt as if an eternity had passed since I'd turned up at HQ hoping to trade a basket full of steaks for one single answer. Now I had more questions than ever, and I might not live long enough to find a single one.

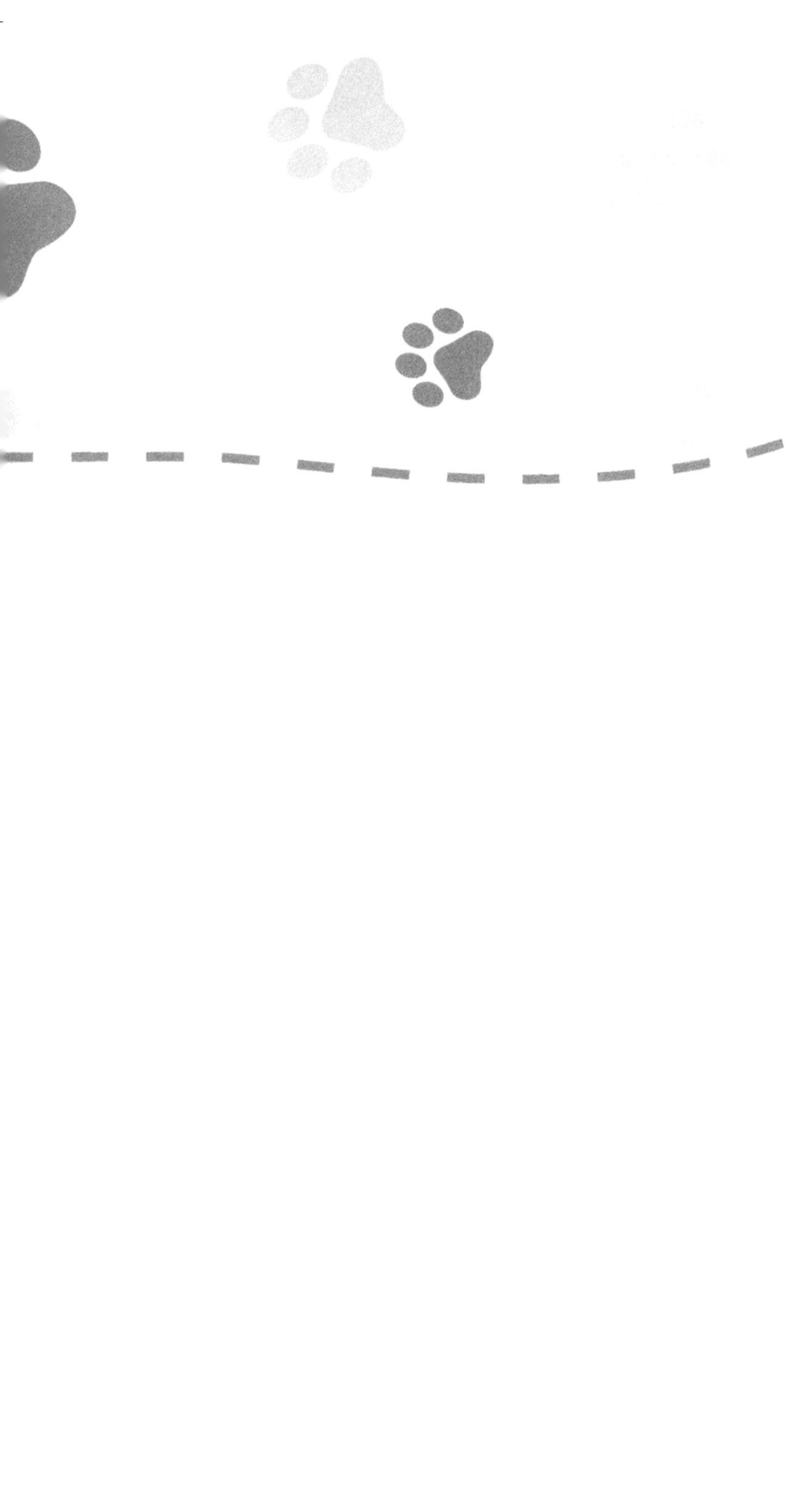

15

arker turned up outside my door at seven on the nose.

"Ready for our big date?" he asked, hope reflecting in his pale eyes. He looked handsome in his navy-blue suit and loafers, but I wished more than anything he'd have stayed home and let me and Connie handle this dispute by ourselves.

He, Melony, and the others would all be liabilities in this fight. While my vampire curse kept me from wanting to protect him because of some misguided emotional attachment, I still didn't want the added obstacle. If he got in the way or messed something up, then I'd be more likely to die myself.

And as Connie was quick to point out, I was a young and inexperienced vampire—not really a vampire at all. We already had the odds stacked against us.

"Well, I'm ready enough for the both of us," Parker said with a dreamy sigh when I failed to respond myself. "You look beautiful, Tawny."

I rolled my eyes. "This isn't a date. It's an assignment. An important one at that."

"Why can't it also be a date?" he asked with a shy smile.

I opened my mouth to answer, but he cut me off.

"I know, I know. You're a big, mean vampire now. But that won't last forever, Tawny. Hopefully, we can end this thing tonight, and you can go back to being you. Then I'll take you out on a real date. One you'll actually want to go on."

"We need to focus on what needs to be done," I reminded him as I sat and yanked a red pump onto each foot. They were the only pair of nice heels I had. I'd paired them with a black high-necked maxi dress, taking care to hide my chest piece beneath. Fluffikins said it would protect me. Connie said the cat was making things up. In the end, it cost me nothing to wear the thing since I couldn't feel pain or discomfort while under the influence of vampire magic. Because of this, I decided to hedge my bets and keep it on until Fluffikins asked for me to return it to him.

I hoped Vanessa wouldn't recognize me out of context, but I also knew that my bubble-gum pink hair had a way of standing out in the crowd. It wouldn't be the worst thing, being recognized. In fact, if the other vampire fixated on me, then it would be easier for Connie to sneak in and take her by surprise.

So either way, I was good to go.

"Mind if I drive?" Parker asked when I grabbed my handbag and stepped out onto the porch.

I motioned for him to have at it. "You might as well."

I could see him going toward the passenger side and used my swift feet to beat him to it. "I've got my own door, thanks."

He just chuckled.

"What's so funny?" I asked when he sank down into the driver's seat and closed the door.

Parker studied me for a moment, then shook his head. "Don't worry about it."

He reached up to jab the key in the ignition, but I clutched his wrist and forced him to look at me. "Tell me."

He sighed and ran a hand through his hair,

messing up the gel job he'd done before picking me up. "It's just you're you, but not. It's like I both have Tawny with me, and I don't."

I quirked an eyebrow and tried not to grin. "So what you're saying is I'm Schrodinger's vampire?"

Parker let out a loud peal of laughter. "Something like that."

"It wasn't a joke," I said, releasing his wrist and then folding my arms over my chest.

"I know," Parker responded as he twisted the key in the ignition and brought the vehicle to life. "I guess it serves me right, huh? I avoided you for days, thinking I was doing the right thing. All I wanted was to keep you safe, but now here you are, Schrodinger's vampire marching to war in high-heeled shoes."

"I make my own choices," I mumbled.

"Now that we're clear on that point, I'll give you many more opportunities to do so," he promised. "Which means you'll be seeing lots more of me."

I shifted toward the window, blocking him out. "No, thanks."

"That's just the vampire talking," he said. "The real Tawny wants that date I offered. There's something special between us. It's been there from the start. And she knows it."

"Yeah, well, I guess that something special between us died when I did," I muttered. It's something I'd been wondering about since Fluffikins gave me this new magic. Was I dead? Undead? Something else entirely?

Parker answered it for me. "You're not dead, Tawny. You're not even undead."

I turned back to face him, but he kept his eyes on the road. "Isn't that what being a vampire means, though?"

"You're not a full vampire," he said firmly. Perhaps for me, and perhaps to remind himself, too. "Just playing dress-up as one for a little while."

"Only if we succeed," I pointed out. "The odds are stacked against us, you know."

"That may be true, but there is no if here. We will succeed."

I cocked my head to the side, considering. "What makes you so sure?"

He glanced toward me with a big, toothy smile and winked. "Because it's the only way you'll agree to that date. Which means I will make sure we win this thing. You can count on me, Tawny. Count on what we have."

Yeah, I guess we'd see about that...

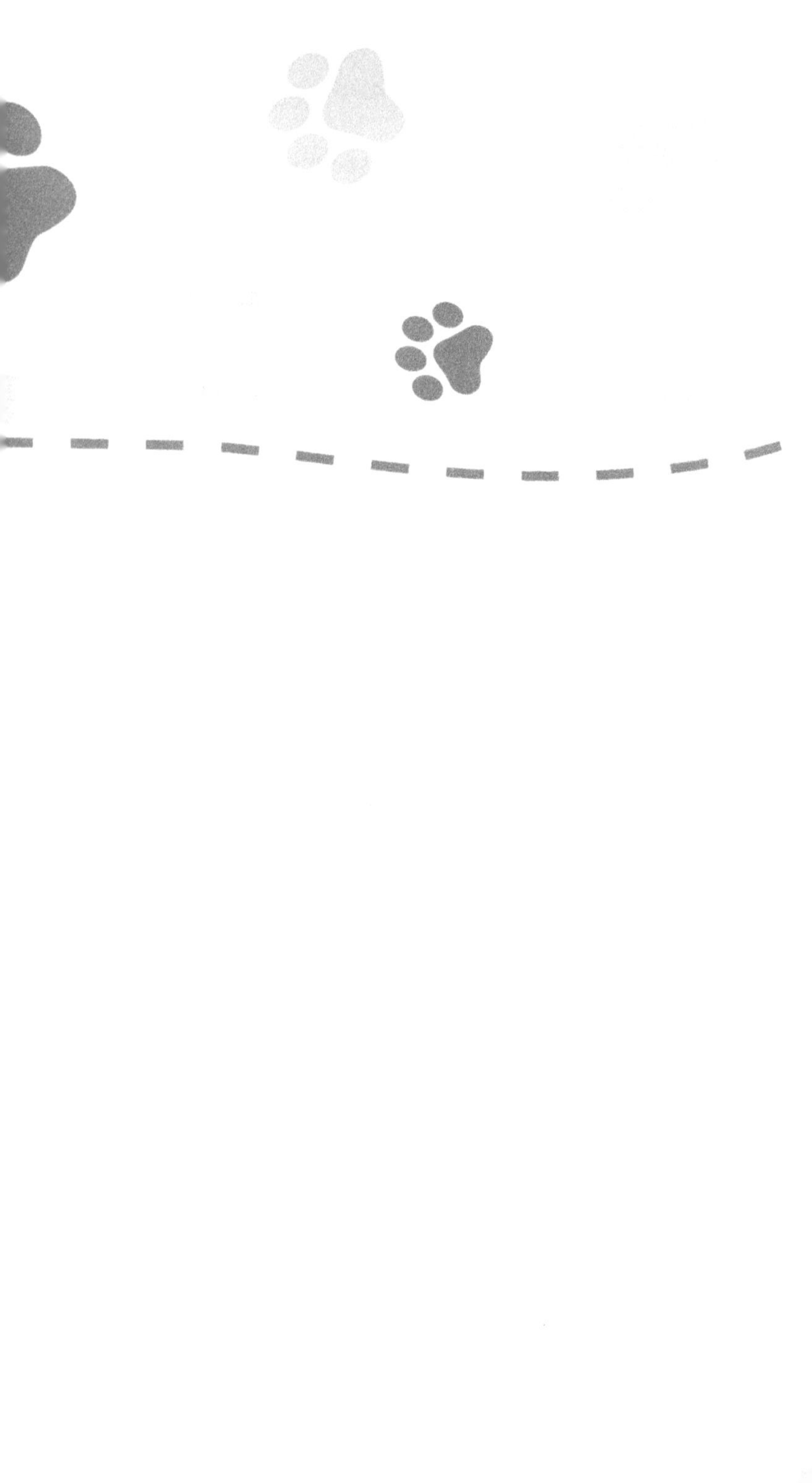

16

Our drive wasn't even three minutes long. One of the reasons I'd decided to rent my cottage was because of its proximity to downtown. I guess Parker wanted to have a getaway car at the ready, which is why he decided to drive us there. He now guided the car into the lot a couple blocks away from Vanessa's restaurant, and the two of us sat waiting in place until Fluffikins appeared in the lot and motioned for us to proceed. I hadn't known we were waiting for his cue, but Parker clearly had.

"Did you get a more detailed rundown of the mission than I did?" I asked, feeling frustrated as we picked our way across the gravel parking lot.

Parker strolled leisurely toward our destination, and I had a hard time forcing myself to keep pace.

"Yes. Fluffikins came by to talk with me this afternoon and share more of the plan that he, Connie, and R concocted back at HQ. From what I understand, he paid a visit to Buckley, too."

"But not me and Melony?" I don't know why I was worried about Melony being left out. I'd hated her well before this vampire curse took hold. Still, fair was fair. And our current predicament was not fair.

Parker frowned. "You and Melony are still very new. It wouldn't be fair to put too much on you."

"But it's fair to leave us out of planning?" I bit back.

"This isn't about what's fair," he whispered as we approached the restaurant and began to mix with other pedestrians on the street. "It's about what gets the job done. Now hold my hand and look like you're happy to be with me."

I laced my fingers through his, despite not appreciating him telling me what to do. He then pulled open the door and held it as I led the way in.

A smiling hostess greeted us. No fangs, which meant she either wasn't a vampire yet or was still too young to have grown into her full powers.

"Welcome to the grand opening of Bollyweird. We offer a bold new take on traditional Indian flavors. Table for two?"

"Please," Parker answered with a matching grin.

The hostess grabbed two menus and led us to a table in the back near the silver buffet I'd spotted during my earlier visit with Connie.

"Looks busy," Parker said, then pulled a chair out for me.

I took a seat, unfolded a cloth napkin, and placed it over my lap. "This place basically appeared overnight. I wonder how they managed to get the word out so fast," I observed as I took in the full house.

"Well, va—I mean, let's say, vegetarians," Parker said with a half-cocked grin. "Vegetarians can be very charming when they want to be. It's easy for them to pull others near."

A chill ran through me. Could I do that, too? And if not now, would I be able to soon? Would I lose myself to this newfound power? I shook my head and whispered, "I'm starting to think there's not much that vegetarians can't do."

"Yes, that's why they're a problem."

"To be honest, I don't see how anyone except me or Connie stands a chance against them."

Parker scoffed at this. "You've been a v... vege-tarian for all of ten hours and already you think you're better than me?"

I picked up the laminated menu and opened it before me. "It's not an emotional thing. I'm simply stating facts here."

"Maybe, but you don't have enough information to reach an accurate conclusion."

The waitress appeared then, notepad in hand. Also not a vampire, I realized. She seemed to have a difficult time navigating the pathways between tables while wearing her deep purple sari with gold trim.

"The lady and I will have the buffet," Parker announced before I'd even had a chance to finish looking over the appetizers. "Provided you have suitable options for vegetarians?"

I kicked Parker under the table while smiling up at the waitress. We had to keep our cover, and he knew that, which is why he was teasing me. *Ugh.*

"Oh, yes. We actually specialize in vegetarian cuisine," the waitress answered in a sing-song voice. "I'll be back around with your waters. Go ahead and help yourselves to the buffet. Enjoy!"

"After you," Parker offered with a smug look of satisfaction.

I rose from the table, working hard not to show how irritated I was with my "date." He followed behind me, even trying to grab my hand, but I refused to let him take it.

We each picked up a plate from the warmer and began to make our way down the serving line. I'd enjoyed feasting on Indian food whenever I found myself in New York or another big city to meet with my editor or host a book signing. Rural Georgia felt like a strange place for a restaurant like this, but who was I to judge? I knew next to nothing about the food business.

I passed over the butter chicken with a sigh. Normally, that was my favorite, but Parker had gone and told the waitress I was a vegetarian, and I would hate to draw suspicion to us over such a small and unimportant detail. So instead, I loaded up on chickpea curry, various paneer dishes, and a massive stack of naan.

Did I actually feel hungry? No.

Was I going to miss an opportunity to stuff my face with such delicious looking food? Not a chance.

As soon as we sat, I tore off a piece of naan and added a spoonful of curry before popping the giant morsel in my mouth.

But the moment the food hit my tongue, I grabbed the napkin from my lap and spit out my entire mouthful.

"Don't eat anything," I whispered to Parker in warning. "Something's wrong with the food."

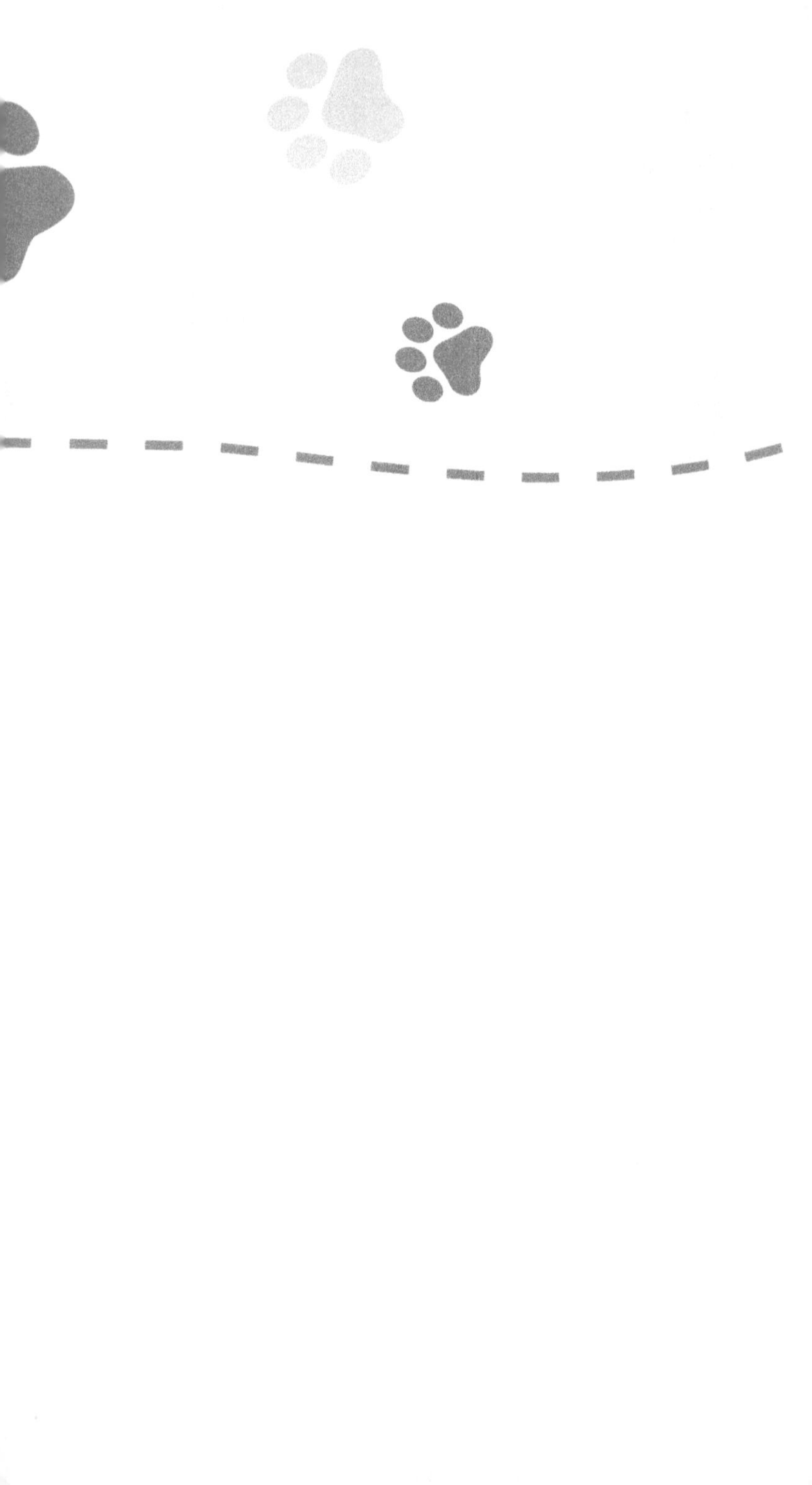

17

"What's wrong?" Parker asked, thankfully setting his spoon down without drawing the compromised food to his mouth.

"Don't overreact..." I leaned over the table to whisper to him. "But I'm pretty sure the food is poisoned."

"How would you know that?" he asked at full volume.

"It tastes..." I rolled my hand at the wrist, searching for the right word.

"Weird?" Parker supplied with one eyebrow raised. "It's in the name, remember? Bolly*WEIRD*."

I shook my head and fell back into my chair.

"No, something's off. I don't know what exactly, but something. I can taste it."

"You haven't eaten yet since becoming a, uh, vegetarian, though, right? Maybe you're just overwhelmed by all the flavors and how they're hitting your enhanced senses," Parker pointed out. I understood his reasoning, but it still irked me that he couldn't just take my word on this. We were losing precious time here.

Remembering what Parker had said about vampires being able to draw people to them, I chose my next words carefully. Could I use my magic to stop all arguments?

"There's something that shouldn't be there. *Trust me.*" I gave that last command extra emphasis, tasting each syllable as it rolled over my tongue.

Parker reached across the table and put his hand over mine. "I believe you," he acquiesced at last. Had I changed his mind with my magic? Part of me didn't want to know. Being able to compel anyone to my will felt like too much power. Perhaps that's why neither Connie nor Fluffikins had mentioned it to me.

I pushed my seat back and stood. "I'm going to the bathroom," I announced, putting on a pleasant smile for anyone who was watching. "See if you can get through to the others," I whispered to Parker before heading off.

He pulled out his phone and immediately began texting. I eyed Buckley seated on the other side of the restaurant with Melony as I made my way toward the bathrooms. He had his phone out and was already studying the screen with a furrowed brow.

With a quick glance back to make sure Parker's attention was otherwise occupied, I slipped past the restrooms and into the kitchen.

The swinging doors announced my arrival with a sudden flourish of movement that drew the eyes of the full kitchen staff.

Well, I'd just found where Vanessa was hiding all the vegetarians—erm, vampires. The four others Buckley had counted all busied themselves at various stations, stirring, braising, baking, and plating. Vanessa stood before a stainless-steel counter chopping an onion at lightning speed.

"I should have turned you away at the door," she muttered, then abruptly stopped dicing and hurled the chef's knife at me. It flew end over end, embedding in the door less than an inch from my ear.

Whoa, I had not been prepared for that. As fast

as I could now move, Vanessa was faster—and she seemed to have zero hang-ups about getting violent.

"That was your warning," the vampire chef hissed. "The next one won't miss."

I took a step back but bumped into the door. Okay, now I was afraid. There was still so much I didn't know about vampires. Would a knife kill me, or did it have to be a wooden stake? And vampire or not, did I even have it in me to chop off someone's head? I was guessing the old garlic trick didn't work, given how much of the spice I'd detected in the food and now saw around the kitchen. So where did that leave me in this fight?

Now that I'd revealed myself, I couldn't back down.

But could I somehow manage to win?

I lowered my gaze and narrowed my eyes at Vanessa, hoping the stance made me appear more menacing than terrified. "What are you putting in the food here? Why are you poisoning the normies?" I demanded, my voice strong and mostly not shaking.

"Who says we're doing anything out of sorts here?" Vanessa answered with a shrug, approaching me with a gentle swing to her hips.

She stopped mere inches before me and raised her hand to grasp the knife beside my head. She didn't pull it out, though. Instead, she leaned in closer. I could smell her stale breath over the other, more pungent aromas in the kitchen.

"What we do to normies is our business. As is this restaurant. It's OUR business, and you're not welcome here. Go. Now." She bit out each of these last words with her glistening fangs on full display.

I could have pushed back through the door, leaving this whole confrontation behind me. Whatever Vanessa hoped to accomplish with her poisoned food, she probably didn't want to create a scene in the middle of the restaurant where all her customers could see. I could have run to Parker or Melony and Buckley, but hadn't I already decided they would only slow me down?

"Connie already asked you nicely," I growled, leaning in even closer. "You know you can't stay in Beech Grove. It's already claimed."

"And I already asked you nicely. It seems both of us have a hard time listening. Huh. Guess that means talking isn't going to get us anywhere."

With that, Vanessa grabbed the chef's knife from the door. I caught the movement and followed it with my eyes, ready to block the attack, but while I was focused on this threat, my opponent withdrew a wooden stake from her apron and shoved it straight into my chest.

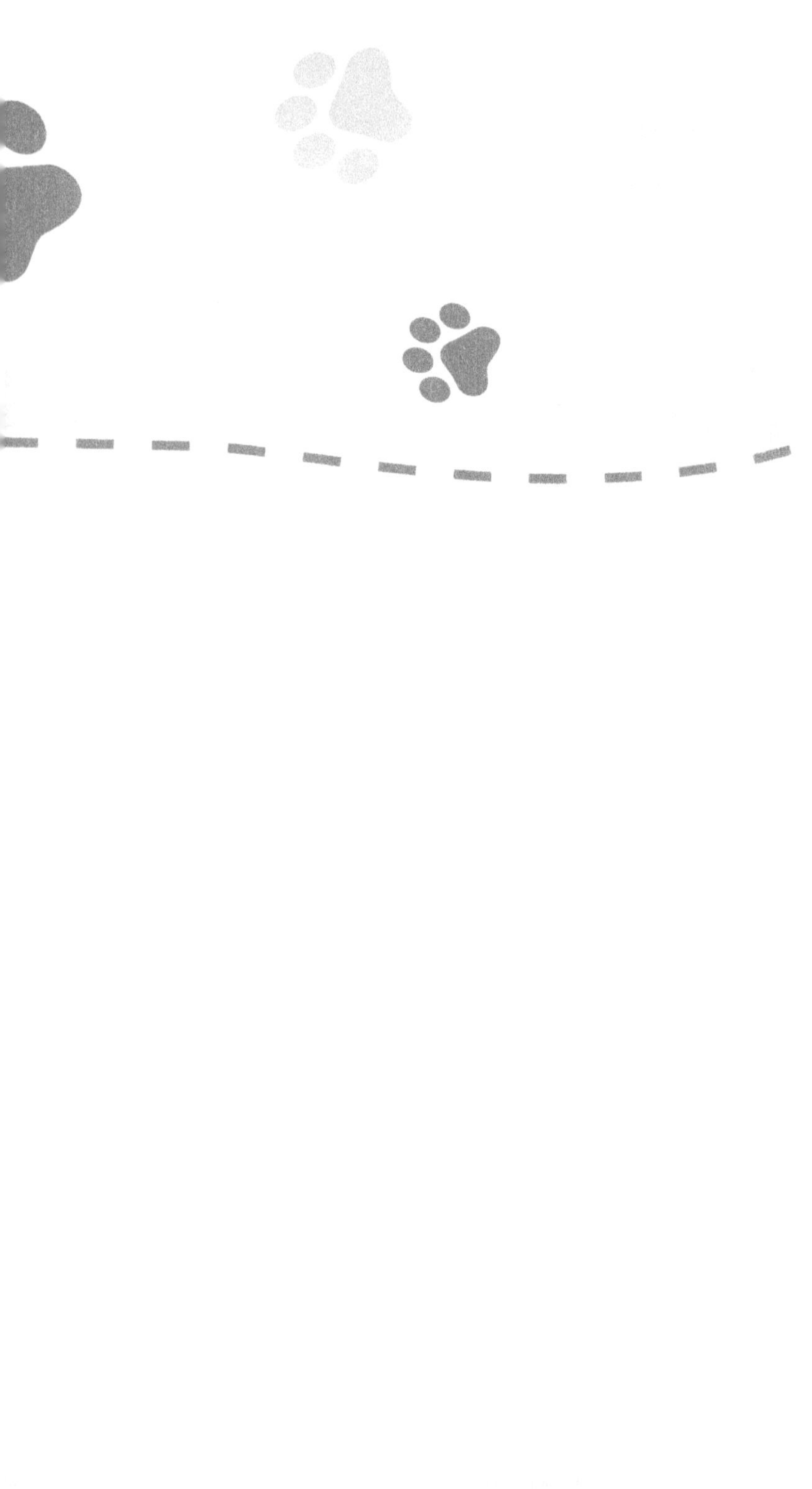

18

gasped in surprise but felt no pain. A stake to the heart should have killed me, right?

My eyes and Vanessa's both shot down to where she held the stake against my chest. The wood had splintered straight up to where Vanessa gripped the weapon in her fist.

It hadn't entered my heart.

The breastplate!

That silly little accessory had held and very likely saved my life in the process.

Our eyes locked and Vanessa swung with her other arm, the one that held the knife. I darted out of the way, unwilling to lose my head or any other appendage. I'd need those when I became human again.

I forgot to adjust for my new strength, however, and hurled myself with too much force, knocking into an industrial stainless-steel dishwasher spewing steam.

No, no, no, no!

I needed to get back to my feet before Vanessa threw herself at me again. I found myself at a distinct disadvantage now. These Bollyweird vampires had the experience, the numbers, and the higher ground.

I was toast.

Or I would have been if the door hadn't boomed open, sending a powerful magical fog swirling through the kitchen. A tall man wearing a dark blue suit and loafers stormed in behind.

Parker!

I wanted to go to him, to clutch his hand, to apologize for thinking of him as a liability, and thank him for saving my life. No, I still didn't love him or anything even close to that. I was, however, incredibly grateful to still have my head attached, to live another day in this crazy world.

One problem, though; I couldn't move. I struggled and strained but couldn't even bat an eyelash.

"Tawny! Tawny!" Parker called as he maneuvered past the vampire chefs, each stuck in perfect stasis.

Much as I wanted to, I couldn't call out in response. Luckily, it didn't take Parker long to find me on the sticky tile floor by the dishwasher.

"Tawny!" he exclaimed, placing a hand to my chest and freeing me from the spell he'd cast.

I let him help me into an upright position even though I didn't need any assistance now that the magical fog no longer trapped me.

He searched me for wounds, his breath panicked, heart wild. "When you didn't come back, I realized you'd probably gone off and tried to take on the coven by yourself. And look, I was right." He smiled at me gently even though his brow remained furrowed with concern.

"How'd you know that?" I asked. I thought I'd had him fooled. That I'd made the perfect plan to give our team the best chance at victory.

"Because I know you. The real you." He raised my hand in his and kissed it.

"Does that mean I'm no longer Schrodinger's vampire?" I asked with a slow grin.

"I don't know what you are exactly. Just that you're pretty spectacular."

"And brave?" I offered.

"I think foolish might be the better word," he retorted. "Seriously, though. Are you all right?"

"I'm fine," I answered, then pounded on my chest plate. "Good as new, thanks to this baby."

He frowned and placed his hand to my chest once again. "Is that what you were wearing earlier today? That collar? What's it for?"

"To keep me from getting staked in the heart, and obviously it worked. Connie should really consider wearing hers more often." I'd been wrong about something important, but so had Connie. Even though vampires were smart and strong, they weren't always right, and they weren't the only ones who had skills of value.

Parker seemed confused. "May I see it?" he asked, sitting back on his heels to give me some space.

"I mean it's kind of under my dress right now, so…"

He flashed a cocky grin, then used his magic to unclasp the armor from behind my neck and untie it from around my waist. A moment later, the armor phased through my dress and floated into Parker's grasp.

"Seems like you have some experience with that," I quipped with an unbecoming snort.

But Parker didn't say anything back. Not even to make a joke.

"Fluffikins gave this to you?" he asked, running his hands over the metal.

I nodded, studying him as he studied the armor. "To protect me."

"No, that's not why." Parker shook his head. "I didn't realize it, earlier in my office. I was too swept away by my feelings to think clearly."

I ignored the feelings part, preferring to focus on the facts—or at least the facts as Parker now saw them. "Realize what? What's wrong?"

"This isn't armor to protect you," he whispered. "It's actually meant to dampen your magic."

I snorted again. "Well, that's ridiculous. I can use my magic just fine."

"Your vampire magic," Parker corrected. "The alloy here isn't meant to drown that out. It's for your witch magic."

Now he had me really confused. "No, I don't have that anymore. Remember? Fluffikins took it back."

Parker helped me to my feet and set the breast-plate aside on one of the kitchen counters. "Did he, though? When's the last time you tried to use it?"

"I haven't tried, because I knew I didn't have it

anymore." I glanced around the kitchen, eyeing Vanessa and the four other members of her coven with hesitation. They may have been frozen in place, but they were still very much alive and angrier than ever.

"Try to use it now," Parker urged, focusing only on me.

I glared down at my hands. Could they still cast magic? Spells?

He raced across the kitchen, eyes still on me. "Here, we can stuff the chefs in this cooler and magically seal it until we're ready to take them in to HQ."

"You want me to do all that?" I balked.

"No, just open the door. One little thing. Now that you're not wearing the dampener you can do it. Tawny, look at me."

He waited until my eyes met his.

"I believe in you," he said, and that was all I needed to hear to believe that his ridiculous assertion might actually be true. That somehow I was a witch and a vampire and me all at the same time.

I took a deep breath and raised my arms...

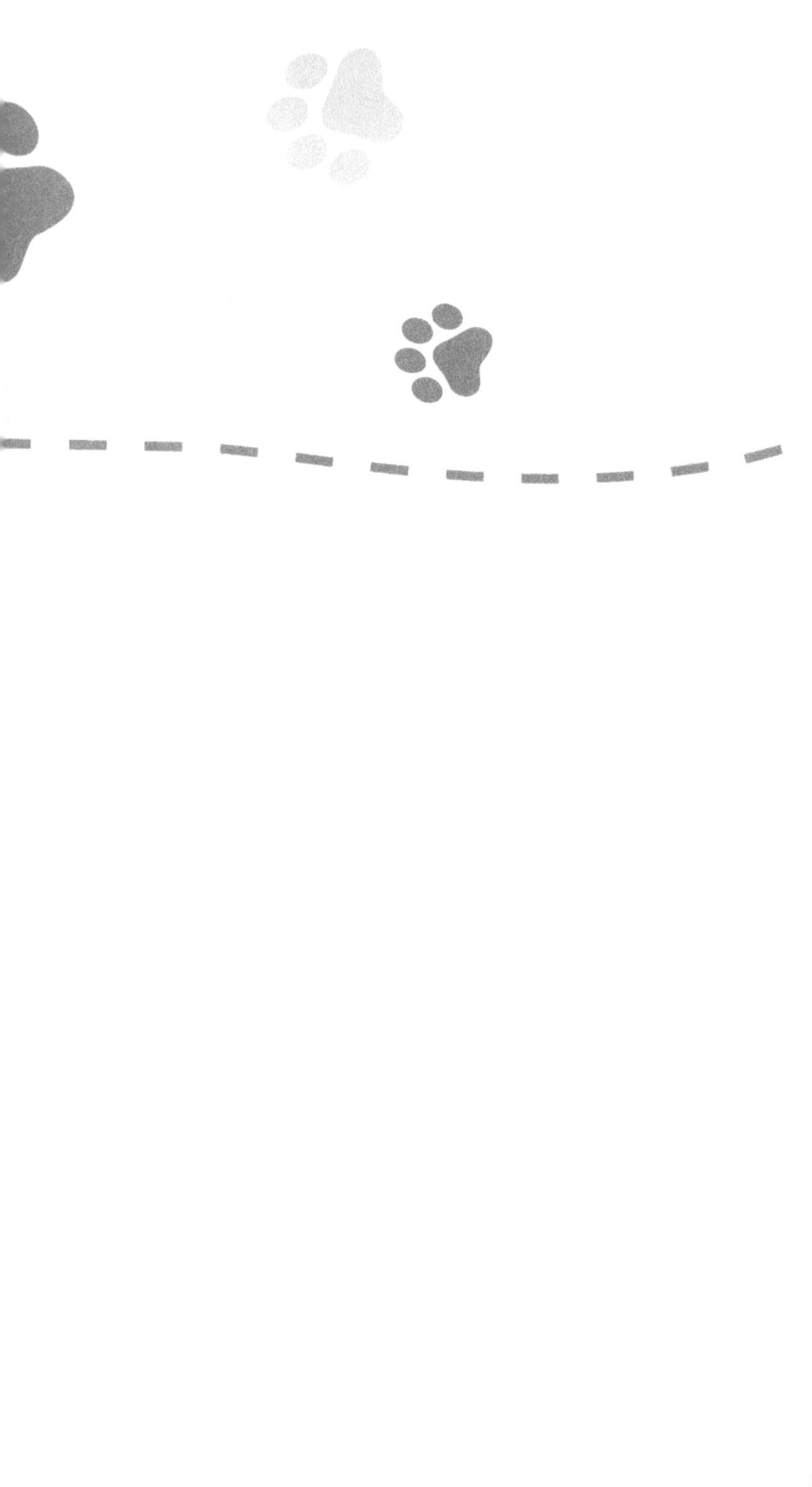

19

The door swung open with unexpected force, banging hard against the wall. I stared into the walk-in cooler with complete amazement. *I did that?*

"Told you," Parker said, running toward me and then taking me in his arms. "You're not a normie, Tawny."

"Then what am I?" I choked out, still unable to believe that I'd kept my temporary witch magic this whole time without knowing it.

"I don't know," Parker murmured into my hair.

"But Fluffikins does." Every muscle in my body tensed. Fluffikins knew what I was and had chosen to keep it from me. Even if not knowing got me killed. He would have to answer for that. I'd make sure of it.

"If he kept it from you, he had his reasons," Parker said, rubbing his hands up and down my arms. "Whatever you are, you're not a full vampire. Which means the curse doesn't affect you in the same way."

"Which means I can still love?" I asked, not certain how I even felt about that anymore. I wanted to want people, but I'd been so focused on getting a handle on my vampire magic and stopping the new coven that I hadn't given much thought to what might happen next for me and Parker.

"Maybe not love." He squeezed my hand and took a slow breath before continuing. "If you kept the witch magic, you might keep the vampire's, too. I don't know what that means, how they'll react to each other long-term. What I do know is, the rules don't apply to you. You're different."

"Yeah, you keep saying that." I bit my lip, wishing so badly I could feel pain in my current form. But no. At least not yet. "So what now?" I asked, afraid of all the answers he might give.

"We take the Bollyweird vampires captive. Figure out why they targeted us. Complete your job.

Make Fluffikins tell you the truth." His words trailed off.

"And then?" My voice hitched.

"I don't know," he answered with a small shake of his head.

We embraced for a few moments longer. It didn't light me up from the inside as it once had, but I found comfort there as I readied myself for what I knew must happen next.

Whether we chose to kill all the members of the outsider coven, hold them captive forever, or simply wipe their memories, a reckoning was coming. Somehow I just knew it deep within my bones.

First the deadly battle for town witch. Then the field agents, Fluffikins, and Melony being kidnapped by a magical mafia in Maine. And now this? Too much was happening too quickly in too small of a rural Georgia town for these events to be isolated coincidences.

Fluffikins knew I was different. Might others, too?

Or were they after something else, and I simply had the dumb luck to get caught up in it all?

I wished I knew...

"Help me round these guys up and jam them in

there," Parker said, letting me go with a beleaguered sigh.

I watched as he wrapped a magical tendril around the first vampire chef and lifted him into the cooler. He then grabbed for another, picking his way through the crew.

I walked over to Vanessa, not far from where I'd left her. She stood with that same chef's knife raised in her hand, head twisted to the side. If Parker had been even a few seconds later, that knife would have found its target. *Me.*

"Why are you here?" I asked her immobile form. "Did you come for me?"

I watched for any sign of recognition, but she was nothing more than a statue while Parker's magic held on to her. He continued to round up the others, I raised my fingers to Vanessa's mouth and let my magic pour from their tips into her lips.

"Why are you here?" I asked our captured foe again.

Vanessa's lips flexed, but her mouth remained closed.

I waved my hand in a circle over her face and neck. Could I use my vampire and witch magic at the same time? There was only one way to find out.

"Tell me," I demanded, attempting my compulsion trick from earlier.

"Why should I tell you anything?" she snarled, then spat at me.

"I can take your life, or I can save it. The choice is yours."

"There are more of us than you can possibly imagine. Killing me will change nothing."

"Do you really value your cause above your own life?"

"What life?" she growled. "You think we enjoy this waifish existence, stuck between life and death? There is nothing for us. No love. No purpose. Nothing but the cause. It gives us purpose. A reason to continue to exist. Anything I tell you could lead you to destroying it. My life is but a small price to pay to protect what so many of us have worked so long for."

"I don't understand," I said with a frown. "None of what you're saying makes sense."

"I don't owe you anything." She laughed viciously. "Silly girl. You don't even know who you are. Do you?"

"Tell me. I need to know," I begged. I didn't care if it made me look weak. In the moment, I was weak. I didn't even know the truth about who I was.

Vanessa opened her mouth to say something but then let out a guttural groan. I watched in horror as a wooden stake emerged from her chest.

"Well, that's one less thing to worry about," Connie remarked before pulling the stake back out of Vanessa and twirling it in her hand. "Let's get the others back to HQ so we can interrogate them."

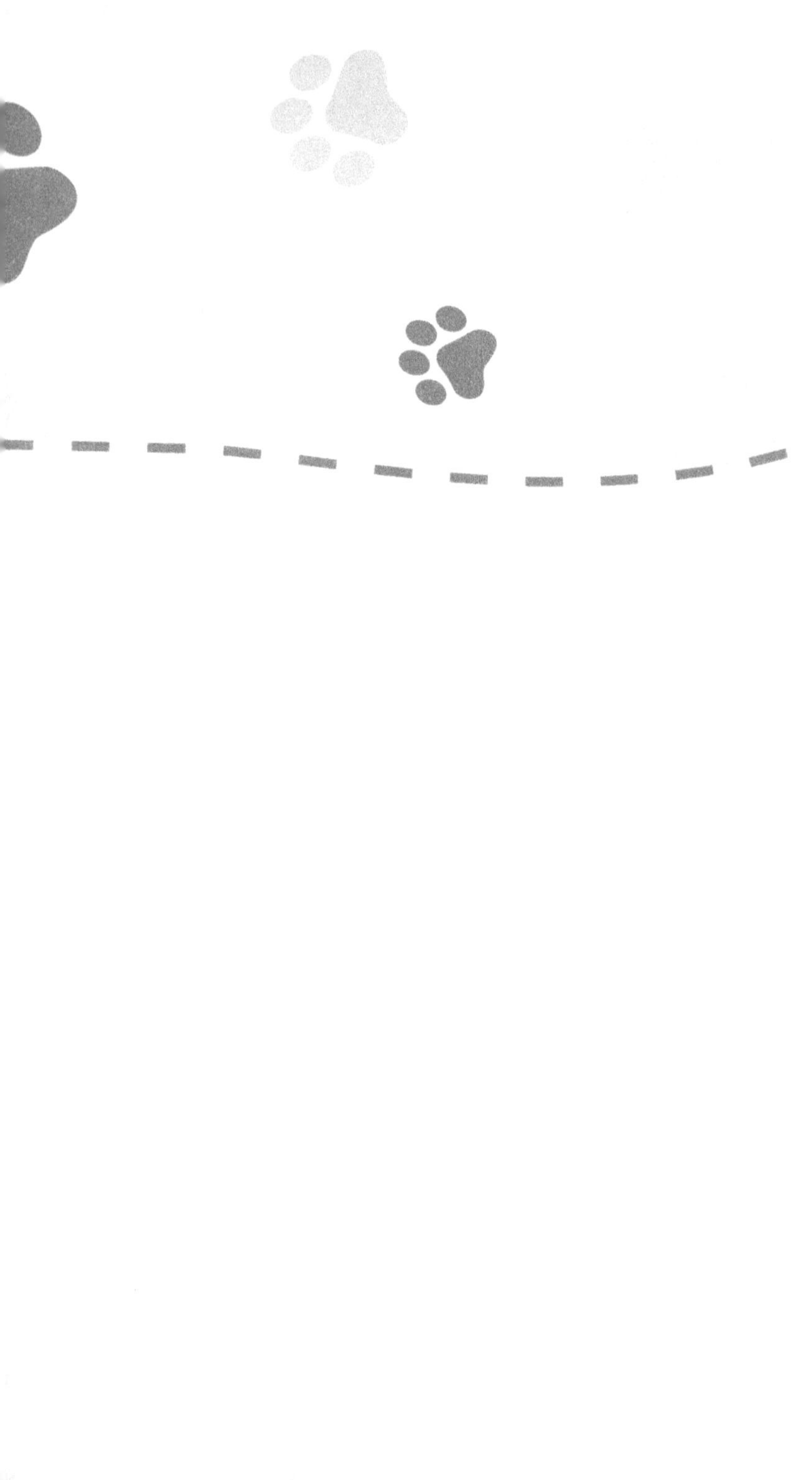

20

"Connie!" I roared in frustration. "I had her right where I wanted her!"

"And now I have her right where I want her. Dead at my feet."

"What was she going to tell me?" I demanded, cursing the poor timing.

"Like I know or care," the vampire responded, shoving her stake into an ankle holster, then popping back up to her full height. "How did you immobilize them all?" she asked me instead.

"P-Parker," I sputtered, searching the kitchen for him.

He let himself out of the cooler, then turned and sealed the door with a bright line of glowing magic.

When he finished creating the seal, he blew on his finger and pretended to tuck it into his waistband.

"Good work, witch," Connie said with an almost-smile.

"Thanks, vampire," he answered back, coming to stand at my side.

"Where are the others?" I asked Connie desperately. Something wasn't right, and it wasn't just the unfortunate timing. "How did you know to come?"

"You made a huge ruckus back here. It took everything the rest of us had to keep the normies from catching wise. Next time, use a little more discretion, huh?"

"The food," I shouted, just now remembering. "They tampered with it somehow."

"Yes, Buckley passed that little bit of news on, too. Next time you need to report directly to your superior."

"You're not my superior," I said, surprising even myself.

Connie's eyes widened so far I thought they might pop out of her head. "What did you just say to me?"

I flicked my wrist and used my witch magic to levitate the dampening armor Fluffikins had bestowed upon me. When it reached me, I grabbed it from the air and handed it over to Connie.

The elder vampire's eyes widened even more. Her mouth dropped open, too.

"How?" she demanded. "You were supposed to have vampire magic."

I darted around her in quick circles, creating a wind that blew her coiffed hair out of place. "I still do."

"But you can't have both at the same time. That would be impossible, unless you were a—" She clamped her mouth shut, refusing to say more.

"Unless I were a what? Tell me!" I yelled.

"It's not my place," she said, turning away from me.

I sent Parker a pleading glance.

"I don't know," he mumbled. "I mean, I'm mortal like you. I haven't lived long enough to amass all the knowledge she has."

"And Fluffikins?" I suddenly needed to know. Who was he really? How had he figured out my true nature before anyone else, and why did he think he had the right to keep it from me?

"He definitely knows," Parker answered.

"But he's not immortal, either. Is he?"

"He's on his seventh life, which makes him well

over one hundred. Plus he's privy to more information than I am as a diplomat."

I considered this for a moment. "Will he tell me?"

"We've defeated the encroaching coven," Connie spoke up. "I believe that means it's time for him to fulfill his end of the deal."

I needed to know, but somehow I dreaded to find out. "What if finding this big secret out changes everything?"

"Everything's already changed," Parker pointed out, wrapping an arm around my waist. I leaned into him, willing to take the comfort wherever it came from. Now that my witch magic was no longer suppressed, I enjoyed his touch again.

"What about the people who ate the poisoned food?" I asked, realizing that almost nothing had been resolved even though we had somehow managed to emerge victorious.

Something was holding me back. I didn't want to leave this place, even though I had no reason to stay.

Connie seemed unconcerned as she sauntered over to the cooler and scowled at the prisoners trapped inside. "We have IDs on all the diners who came in and out tonight. As our head of Agriculture, I'm sure Buckley can figure out what the poison was meant to do and find a way to counteract it."

"I'll get the others in here," Parker said, pulling his phone out of his pocket and beginning to text even as he spoke. "They can help us escort our guys in the cooler to HQ."

"What about the customers who are still in the restaurant?" No, we couldn't leave yet. I didn't know why, only that it was important.

"Easy," Melony said as she pushed through the swinging doors. She must have been standing right there, waiting to be called in.

Rather than explaining herself, she sent a plume of fire into the air. Everyone watched as it hovered near the ceiling.

And then the sprinklers went off, and shocked cries rose up from the dining room.

"That should send everyone outside," Melony said with a huge grin. She clearly loved causing mischief.

"Let's move fast," Connie said, "before the front-of-house staff comes back in and starts searching for the owner."

"Melony, help me guide the hostages out of here," Parker called over to the only person who had less seniority than me. "They're already magically bound. We just need to make sure no normies see until we can stuff them into our cars and out of sight."

Melony nodded and moved toward the cooler to join him.

Those two set to work while Connie hoisted Vanessa's prone body into her arms. "I'll dispose of this one."

"And I'll grab some food to go so I can reverse engineer the poison and create the antidote," Buckley added. I hadn't even noticed him come in, yet there he was.

That left me as the only one without a job. I stood in place and watched as the others got to work.

I didn't want to leave, even though I had no reason to stay.

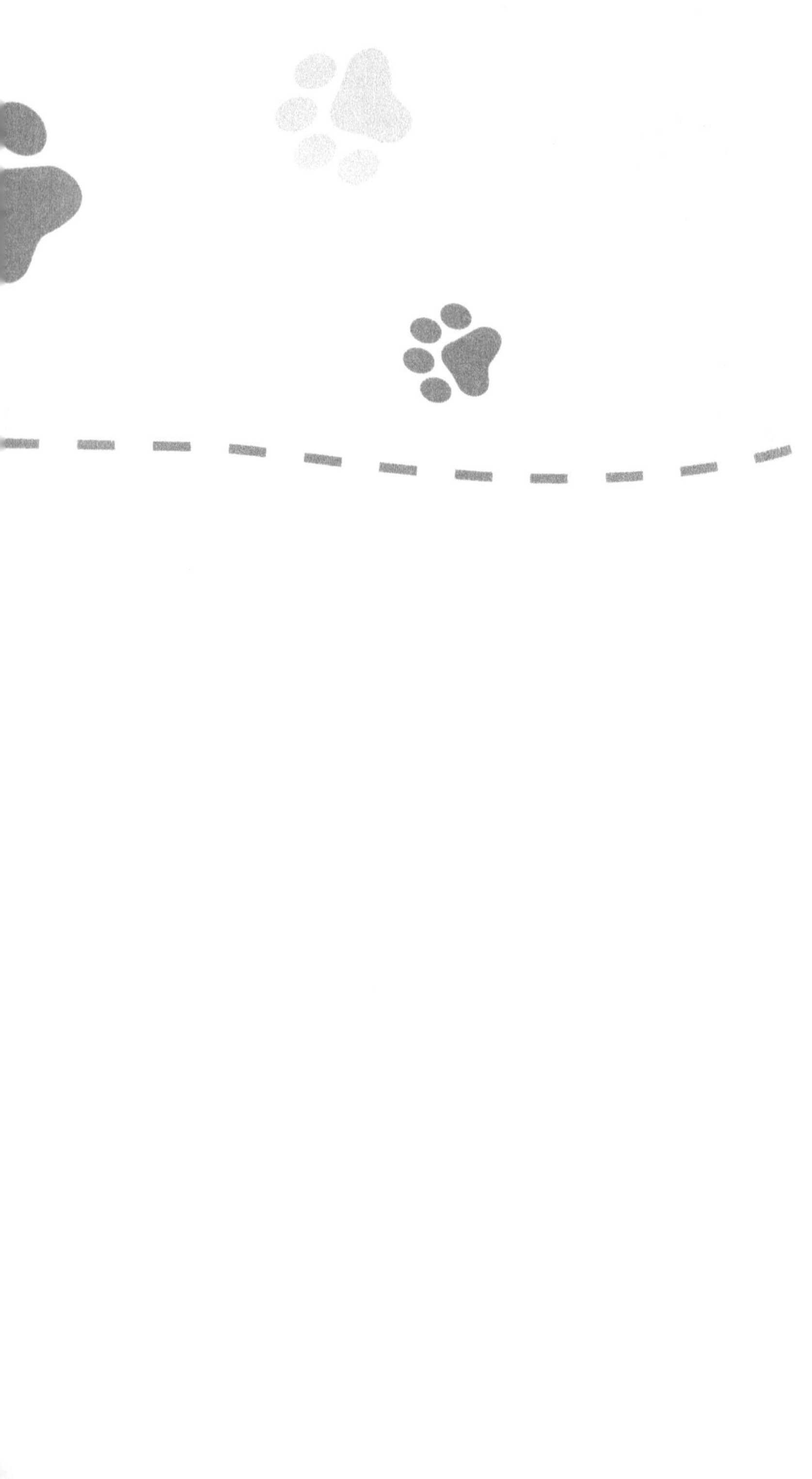

21

I paced the empty kitchen, wondering why I couldn't bring myself to leave. My thorough investigation of every cabinet, cupboard, and drawer came up empty. Nothing appeared out of sorts. But it sure felt that way.

Before Connie had killed her, Vanessa promised we hadn't seen the last of our enemies, of those who adhered to some unnamed cause.

And I believed her.

I just wished I knew more. That I could have compelled her to say more in her final moments.

A flash of black caught my eye as Fluffikins slipped in through the swinging doors.

"Come, Tawny," he urged. "There's nothing more to be done here."

"Something's going to happen," I told him without any hesitation. I felt so sure we weren't done here yet even though I had no obvious reason to feel that way. Still, my intuition gnawed at me.

Fluffikins turned toward the door and motioned for me to follow. "Barnes just delivered them to HQ for questioning. They're safely secured. It's over."

I shook my head, refusing to budge. "I don't think it is."

"If there is to be a round two, we'll be ready," he promised while waiting for me at the door. "But for now we rest."

I shook my head and took a step back. Why was I so resistant?

The black cat sighed. "Don't you want to know why you're different? You've completed your end of our bargain. It's time for me to finish mine. Come. There is much we need to discuss."

I glanced toward the cooler where Parker had temporarily kept the captured coven members. Already I knew they wouldn't talk, no matter what tactics the PTA tried to use against them. Like Vanessa, they would gladly die for their cause without revealing a single hint as to its purpose.

"This job is over, but you're still my temp." The boss's patience had worn very thin, and his words came out rough. "Come with me. That's a direct order," the cat said with a flick of his tail.

At last I gave in to his wishes. Whatever business I still had in this place, it hadn't revealed itself to me yet. Maybe I was just being silly.

"Pick me up," the boss cat ordered when I joined him at the door.

I did, and a moment later, a sparkling pink fog wrapped around our bodies and teleported us back to the conference room at HQ. After delivering us to our seats, the swirling magic began to recede toward the ceiling.

"Stay," Fluffikins commanded, and the magic rearranged itself into a tight sphere, hovering above the table as if it, too, had a seat in this meeting.

I knew very little of the special magic that tied our region to the others in the world. Only that they all drew from the same source and helped maintain balance, keeping any one region or person from growing too powerful.

"Will the others be coming?" I asked, wishing I had Parker at my side for whatever came next. He had my best wishes at heart, but I still didn't know whether the black cat or any of the others did.

"This is a private matter. The fewer who know what I am about to tell you, the safer we will all be."

Fluffikins's eyes appeared dull, whereas usually they shone bright and inquisitive. Whatever he had to tell me, he clearly didn't look forward to saying it.

"What's wrong?" I asked, sucking in a nervous breath and holding it inside.

"You, Tawny. You're what's wrong."

I scoffed at this. Hadn't he agreed to play it straight now that I'd finished my latest assignment? He'd seemed so eager to get me here, and now this.

"That's a terrible thing to say," I grumbled, exhaustion finally sinking in. "I've done everything you've asked of me." Was he only going to speak in riddles and half-truths rather than directly revealing what I needed to know?

"You misunderstand me. What I'm saying is you shouldn't exist."

I swallowed hard as my heart sped up in my chest. When had it even started beating again? So much had happened since Parker removed my dampening armor. I hadn't paid attention to these physical sensations, just assuming they were still absent. But now I felt my heart thrumming, the swell of oxygen in my lungs, the pain of Mr. Fluffikins's words.

"Are you going to kill me?" I asked him point-blank.

Rather than pacing as he normally did, the cat lay down and tucked his front paws under himself. "No, Tawny, I'm not going to kill you. But others will likely try if they ever find out what you are. We can't let them. Do you understand?"

I thought back to my final confrontation with Vanessa. "They already know," I said with a quiver in my voice. "The head vampire told me. Said I don't even know what I am. That others would come."

Fluffikins moaned long and loud. "Then it's exactly as I feared."

"I don't understand. I didn't even know magic existed until a little over a week ago. Why is everyone so concerned about me now?"

"You're not a normie," the cat said, staring at me with large, unblinking eyes.

"Yeah, I've kind of gathered that I'm a magick by now." I let out a chuckle to ease the tension in the room. My attempt at levity, however, only increased the cat's anxiety.

He licked his paw several times—a nervous tic —before speaking again. "No, Tawny. You aren't a magick, either. You're something else altogether."

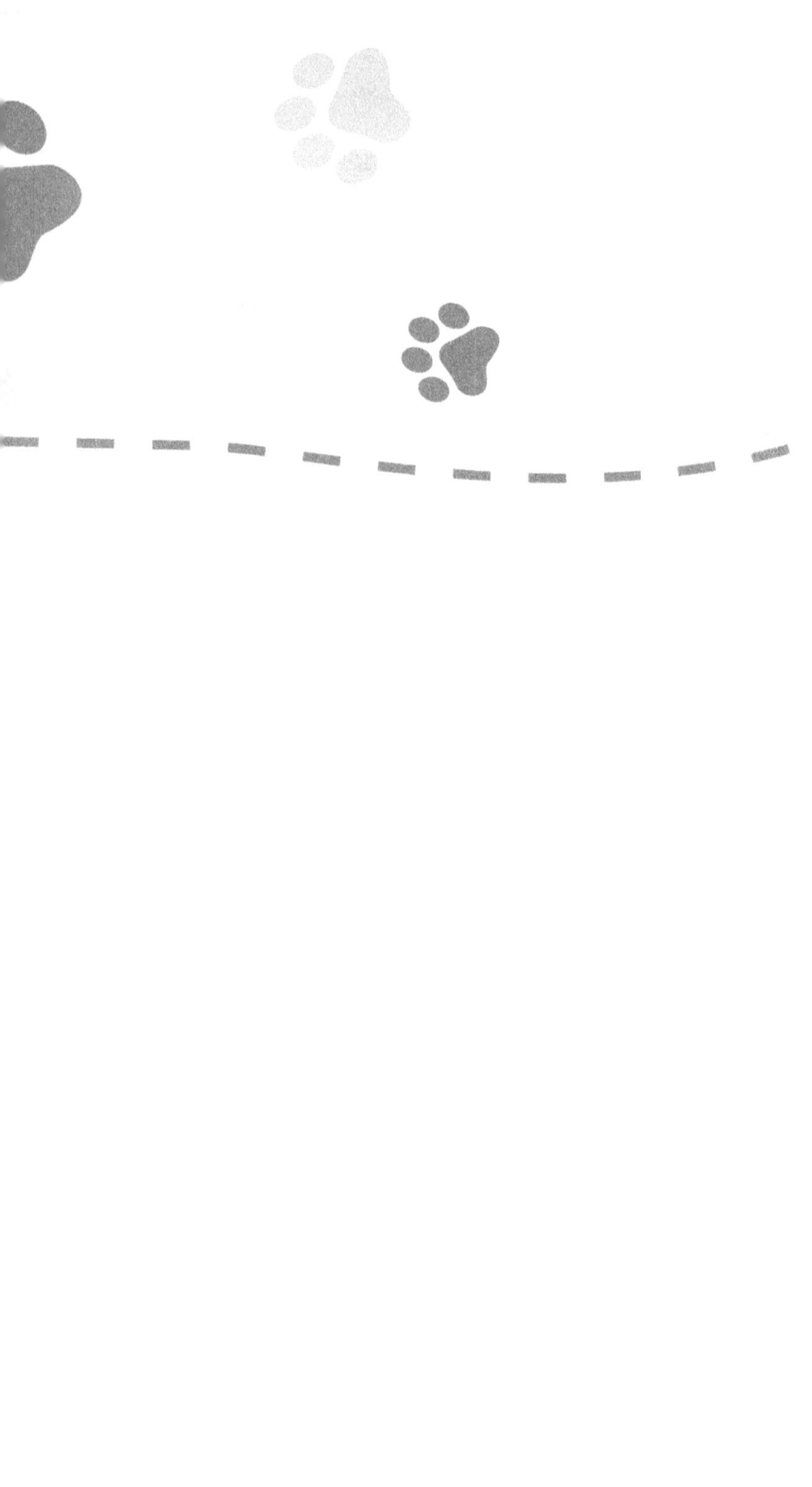

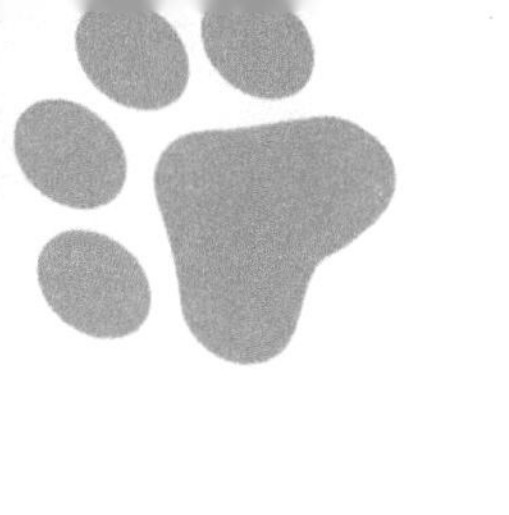

22

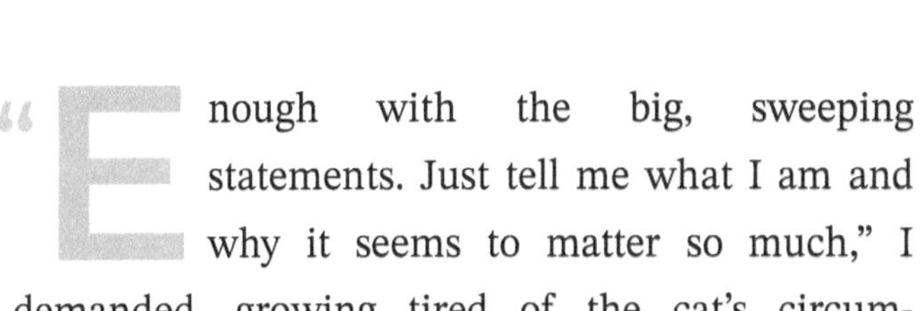

"Enough with the big, sweeping statements. Just tell me what I am and why it seems to matter so much," I demanded, growing tired of the cat's circumlocution.

"You're a Terran," he answered in an eerie monotone.

"A Terran?" I let out a dry laugh and slapped the table. "Isn't that what humans are called in science fiction novels? Please just be honest with me. I've waited long enough to—"

"I am being honest with you!" he bit out. "Terrans are extinct, or at least everyone thought they were, until..." He raised his chin and widened his eyes.

I lifted a hand to my chest. "Until me?"

"Yes. They were spoken of often in old stories. When they went extinct centuries ago, normies no longer had any frame of reference to understand the Terran kind. They saw their frequent mentions in connection to the world and assumed they couldn't find any Terrans, because all on Earth were of this species. But they got it wrong."

"What am I?" I asked hardly above a whisper.

"You are a class to your own. As you continue to interact with the magical world, your powers will only grow."

"But in Caraway Island, I was able to rescue you and Melony because I was a normie. No magick could break through the barriers, but I could," I reminded him, thinking back to that strange adventure. How in the end, I'd been the only one capable of mounting the rescue.

"You're not a magick, and you're not a normie. Since Terrans were thought to be extinct, they didn't account for them when erecting their defenses."

"So I'm magic, but not magick?" I asked. Wow, I really was Schrodinger's something.

He nodded and licked his paw again. "Think of it this way. Most magic users channel their powers through their hearts. That's why vampires can only be killed by destroying the source of their magic—the heart."

"You gave me the chest piece to cover my heart and block my witch magic," I realized, understanding his ruse better and better as more was revealed.

The cat nodded again. "I had my suspicions about what you were, but I also knew you were too unpracticed to have full command of your abilities. When you wouldn't stay away, I thought I might instead keep you hidden in plain sight. Tawny, a Terran doesn't just store magic in her heart. Your entire body is a vessel. You can hold so much power inside you. Hundreds of times what most magicks can. But your real strength is in the ability to wield the world magic."

My eyes snapped to the glowing pink ball coiled beside us.

"Yes," the cat said with reverence. "When the last known Terran died, we erected regional boards to oversee the world magic. We figured that in the absence of its true keeper, the world magic would best be served by a board of supernaturals from multiple classes. Together, we hoped we could approximate the abilities of a single Terran. But it's been an imperfect solution, and both normies and magicks fight more than they were ever meant to. The world isn't balanced, but maybe it can be again, now that we've found you." He paused to let the weight of his words sink in.

Not only was I magical. I was the most powerful being to live for centuries. Being just a little bit special I could handle, but being so above and beyond everyone else? It terrified me.

"Not everyone wants peace," I muttered, thinking of the mainstream politicians and fringe terrorist factions who both pushed war, violence, and discontent with seemingly every breath.

"Not those who seek power, no." Fluffikins's tail now beat against the table as if keeping time. As hard as this conversation was on me, I could tell it hit him just as deeply. He knew much better than me what my existence and discovery could mean for the world at large.

"Does that mean they'll try to kill me?" I squeaked.

The cat nodded glumly. "Yes, or capture you for use as a weapon."

No, I refused to be changed, to be turned into something I was never meant to become. "What can I do to stop either of those things from happening?"

"I do not know. We are in uncharted territory here. No one thought it was possible, but if you're here, then there could be others, too."

"Does that mean we need to go find them? Bring them to our side?" Surely, we had to do something. But what? If Fluffikins didn't have the answer, there was almost no chance I'd be able to find it myself.

The cat sucked in a deep breath before continuing. "I intend to train you in each branch of magic and hope you'll have a way of finding other Terrans, yes. But it won't be easy. We got lucky in finding you before anyone with ill intentions could. It's truly a one in one trillion coincidence, unless there are others out there, just waiting to be discovered."

"I want to help find them," I said with a jolt of enthusiasm. It was too much pressure, being the only one of my kind, especially since the way Mr. Fluffikins explained it, the Terrans wielded a great deal of power and influence. I'd only ever really been responsible for myself. I'd never even had a pet for goodness' sake.

Fluffikins seemed to sense the fear that lay

beneath my determination. "The board and I will teach you everything we know, but your training will be imperfect. We can only teach what we know, which is so little compared to what you will need to learn."

A part of me wished I could go back, could choose a town other than Beech Grove. But if the world needed a hero, I guess I'd have to do.

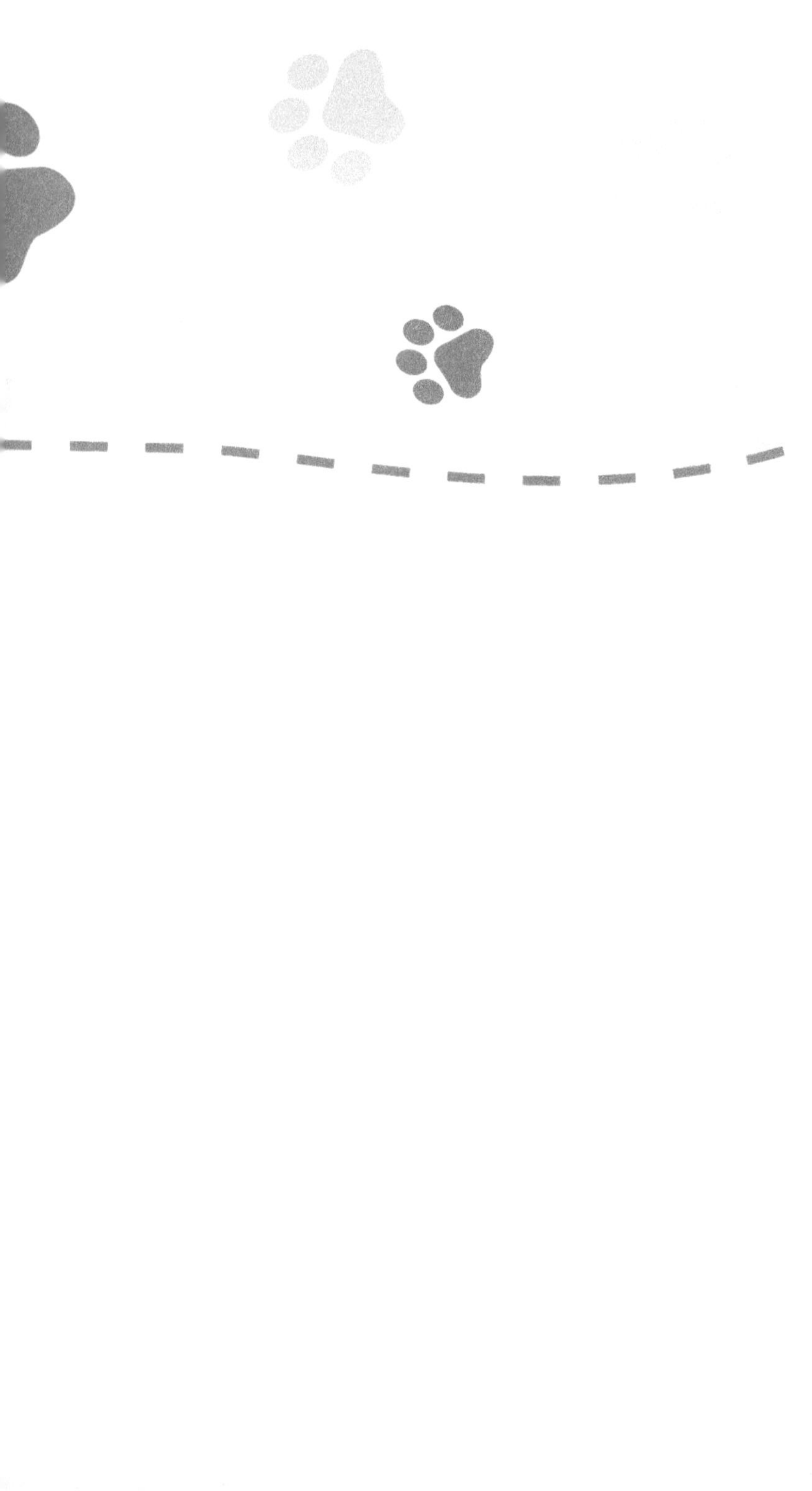

23

"This is a lot to take in," I said when it seemed Mr. Fluffikins had run out of warnings to give.

He stood and stretched. "I know. I wouldn't wish it on anyone. Because of what you are, every single choice you make could change the entire course of history."

"You're not making it any easier on me," I told him with a tired smile. He hadn't been keeping the secret to irritate me. He really had hoped to protect me. Now that I understood, I felt grateful for his efforts.

"I had hoped you would fail and be forced to remain a vampire," he admitted now.

"I will remain a vampire. Well, at least in part," I

said thoughtfully. I still didn't know how this all worked, but I was beginning to see patterns emerge. "The witch magic you gave me hasn't left. The vampire magic won't, either. I absorb it all and keep it inside."

The black cat chuffed. "Like a sponge."

I nodded. "Yeah, and I have no idea how to get rid of it."

"I think I might," Fluffikins revealed, slowly rising to his feet. "The vampire curse was my last-ditch attempt to save you from what you are. I didn't know if it would work, if the curse could erase your Terran heritage, but I had to try."

"I understand that now. Thank you." I didn't always appreciate his methods or attitude, but at least now I saw where he was coming from. At the end of the day, Mr. Fluffikins was just a simple cat who suddenly found himself with far more power than he'd ever expected to wield. We were the same in that way.

He paced to the far corner of the table, then turned back toward me. "It's time we stop denying what you were born to be. We need to unite you with your purpose."

The glittering pink orb of world magic floated across the table, drawing close to me.

"Reach out and take it," the cat commanded from a few strides away.

I raised my hand and extended my index finger. I didn't take any time to think or consider the implications of accepting such a huge responsibility. In my bones, I knew this was right. Necessary.

The orb began to pulse as it moved forward and gently lapped into my skin. I watched in amazement as its rosy glow spread over me, not just settling in my heart like the other magics that had come before but filling my whole body.

Fluffikins gasped. "In all my lives, I never thought I'd see such a sight. You're... incandescent."

When the vampire magic had been dominant in my system, I felt a constant absence, emptiness. Holding the world magic inside me now, I felt the exact opposite—whole, complete, able to feel every sensation that competed for my attention.

And it was wonderful.

"How do you feel?" Mr. Fluffikins asked, examining me with awe.

"Right," I murmured in awe. "Like this is the way it should have always been."

An enormous smile stretched between his whiskers. The first I'd seen from him in quite some time. "Do you remember how we tested the curse earlier today?"

"Parker," I said with a wistful grin. Remembering the feelings I'd developed for him over the past couple weeks, I now yearned for him with renewed intensity. Was I making up for lost time? Or did everything burn more brightly now that I had stepped away from the vampire curse and back into the light?

"I can bring him to you, see if the curse is removed to your satisfaction. However, you can't tell him what you are. You can't tell anyone." He plopped his rear on the table, daring me to argue with his decree.

And what he asked was huge. How could Parker and I grow our relationship if this huge part of me had to remain a secret between us? "Won't he be in danger protecting me? Won't all of you be in danger?"

"Unfortunately, yes, but they'll be far safer if they don't know the exact nature of what you are." Fluffikins tilted his head to the side and mewed. I'd never seen him look so much like an actual cat before. Was this his way of communicating regret or pity? Or had he simply grown weary of me, of this conversation, of what we both knew would come next?

"Connie knows," I said, bringing this strange moment between us to an end. "She figured it out at the restaurant."

He sighed and hung his head. "You are the strongest of us all. You can wipe her memory if you choose. You could even clear mine."

"No," I said and then realized something strange and startling. "I trust her. But I agree not to tell the others."

"Very well then, but if you change your mind, you know what to do."

I nodded, feeling the weight of this new responsibility deep down. I'd never been anyone special. I'd always just done enough to get by. But now?

Now I was the most important person on the entire planet.

I kind of wished I could tell my ex-husband and his new wife, just to rub it in their faces, but I had far more important things to worry about now.

"I'll send Barnes in," Fluffikins said. "But first you need to control your glow. This is supposed to be a secret, remember?"

A secret. Yes.

Keeping it would not be easy.

Though it would be vital.

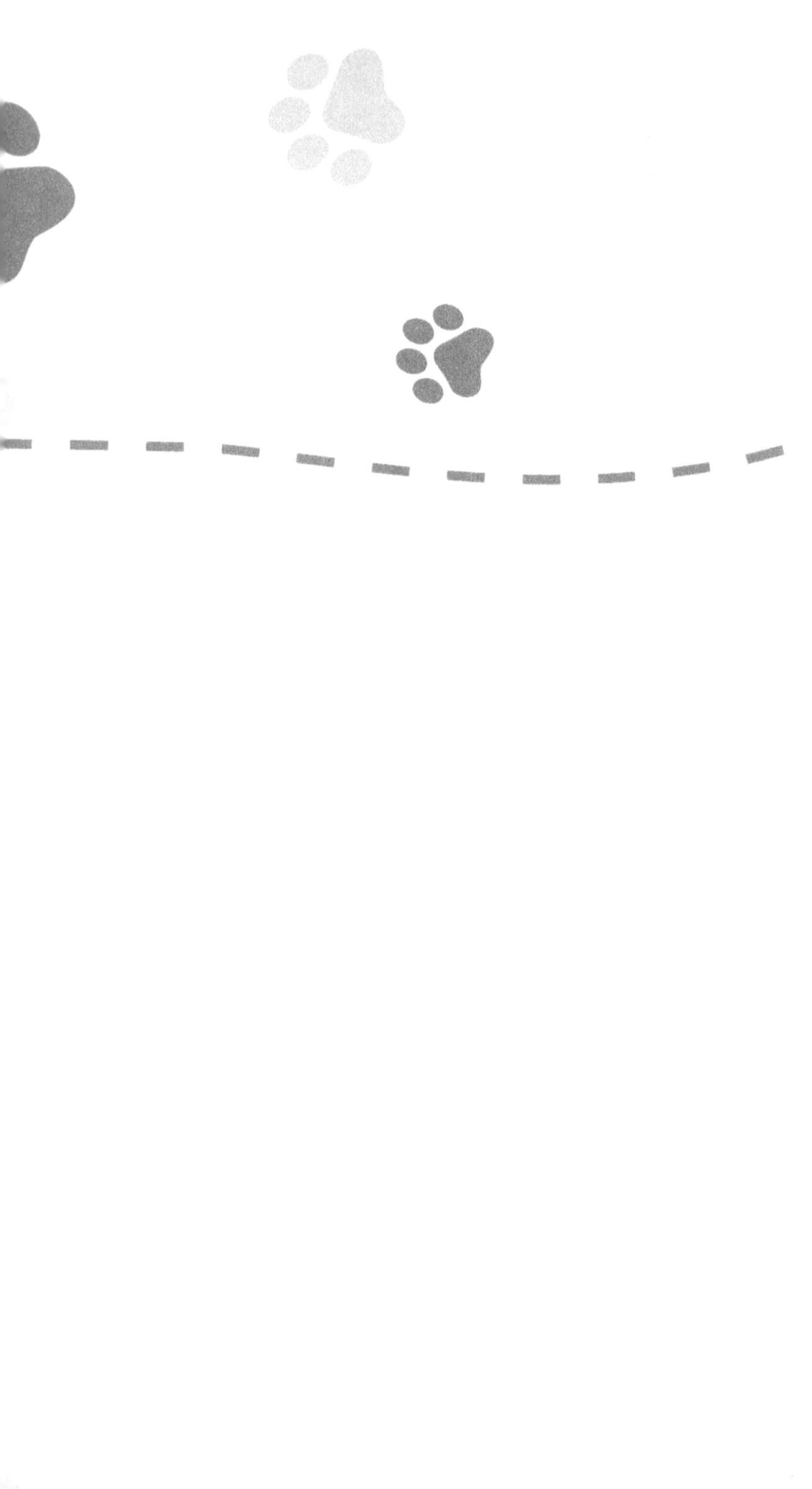

24

arker appeared a few minutes after Mr. Fluffikins left the conference room. Thankfully, I'd quickly managed to tame the powerful new force within me. The added pressure of a deadline seemed to help. I wondered if that would be important later. I'd have time to figure it all out when the moment was right. Not much time, but it would have to be enough.

"Is everything okay?" Parker asked as he pulled out a chair beside me. "The boss cat sent me in. Did he tell you what's going on?"

I nodded, afraid to meet his eyes in light of the lies that would be coming. That was another thing Fluffikins had left to me, coming up with an explanation that would minimize any further questions.

"My witch magic didn't go away because it's my natural magic," I explained, preferring not to hide my magical nature completely. "Joining the PTA awakened what was already in me."

Waves of joy undulated from his chest and crashed into me. I could not only feel my emotions now, but his, too. And I didn't even have to look to know he wore a giant smile on his face. How many new abilities would I discover? Did I even have any limitations left at all?

"Tawny, that's fantastic! You're like me. Our magics match."

I let out a soft laugh. "Yeah."

"Did Fluffikins already take back your vampire magic, then?"

I nodded. "He also wants to keep me around for a while longer to help me get a hold on my new abilities." Well, at least that part wasn't a lie.

The soft gray eyes that had initially sparked my attraction to Parker now shone with happiness. "Seriously, this is perfect," he continued, not realizing that my mood didn't match his own. "I don't have to try to protect you, and I don't have to worry about your safety anymore. You're not a helpless normie stuck in a world of magic. Now you can take care of yourself."

Now this, this I didn't like. "I could always take care of myself. And I was never helpless."

"Sorry, sorry, you're right. I apologize for my misguided chivalry, but I promise that's the last you'll see of it. Oh, Tawny. I'm so happy. I wanted to date you, anyway, but now that our magics match, so many things will be so much easier." He pulled me to my feet and wrapped his arms around me.

"That is good news," I said, forcing a smile. He had no idea that our situation had gotten so much worse. But if I told him, I'd be putting him in the direct line of fire.

He raised his hand to caress my cheek, and I leaned into it. "May I try to kiss you again? Since last time didn't... Well, you know."

Yes, I wanted this. I wanted him. Even though now I would be the one keeping myself at a distance to protect the other.

I tilted my head up and closed my eyes, and a moment later his lips found mine—soft, gentle, and searching for answers.

Yes, I wanted him. Needed him. Even in a crazy new world that seemed so wrong, I knew Parker was right for me. We were just getting started, but already he elicited feelings in me that I had never felt with my ex-husband.

Joy. Trust… Hope.

Hope that Fluffikins's grim predictions for the future would not come to pass, that one day this man and I could live out our happily ever after.

But our story was just getting started, and we still had many monsters to slay.

I pulled back and placed a hand on Parker's chest.

"Did you feel anything?" he asked, studying me carefully.

"I felt many things," I teased. "And they were all right."

He let out a quick sigh of relief and then kissed me again.

"Your curse. It's gone! I don't know what I would have done if you stayed a vampire, Tawny."

"Well, now you don't need to worry about that anymore," I said, holding back the fact that what I actually was might be even worse. I'd just been entrusted with this secret, and already I wanted to share it with him. Wanted to but couldn't.

Ugh. I needed to change the topic.

"Did you finish questioning the vampire chefs?" I asked casually before realizing that this was, in fact, a very good question to ask. With the world magic coiled inside me, I might be able to get them to talk, to tell me things they hadn't told the others.

Sure enough, Parker pressed his lips into a firm line and took a deep, doleful breath. "Not a peep out of them. I'm not sure what we're going to do. Connie wants to stake them all, but what if they didn't know what Vanessa had planned? What if they're innocent in all of this?"

"Can I talk to them?"

He shook his head. "It won't do any good. They're pretty firm in their decision not to talk to us."

I placed a gentle hand on his arm. "It will do me good. Even if they don't say anything, I'll feel better knowing I've tried."

Parker leaned in and placed a kiss on my cheek. "I love your determination. You've really taken all this magic stuff in stride."

I laughed at that. Seriously, he had no idea.

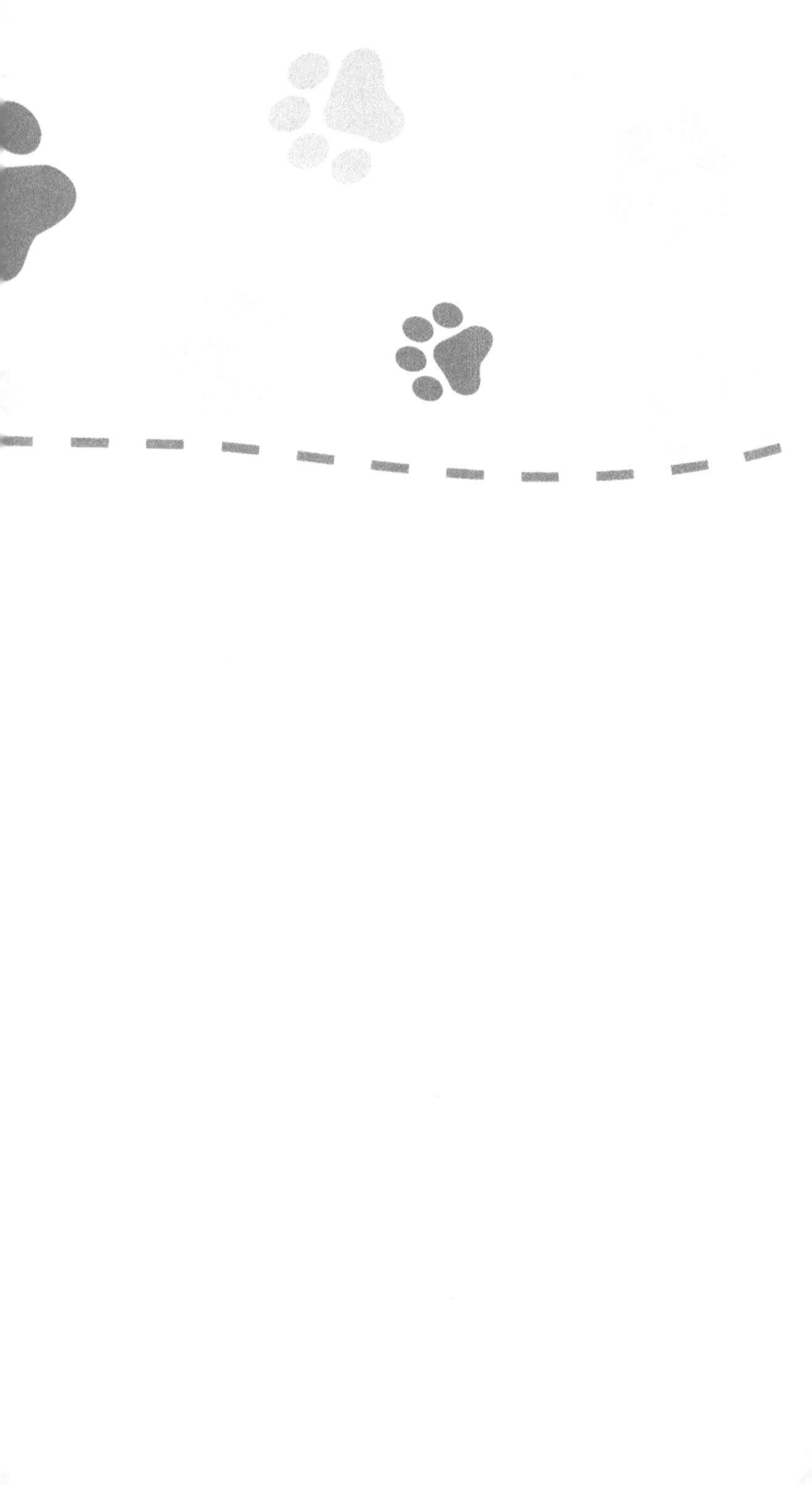

25

arker held my hand as he guided me toward the warehouse-like room where Fluffikins kept his stash of magical artifacts hidden in a special ceiling hold.

We walked right up to the opening in the ceiling, but instead of looking up, Parker looked down. He tapped his foot four times, then moved a couple paces to the side and tapped it twice more. He moved and tapped again, then one last time with a single stomp.

And a section of the hard floors disappeared, revealing a long, dark staircase.

"Has this been here the whole time?" I asked in disbelief.

He flashed me a grin and then motioned for me

to go down ahead of him. The steps lit up beneath me with a magical glow to guide our descent.

We walked for a long time, at least forty steps deep, until finally we came upon a hidden room that appeared to be carved from one giant slab of stone. A magical sheen separated the far corner, cutting diagonally to create a small, triangular cell where four prisoners sat.

"Are you sure about this?" Parker asked one more time. "You'll be safer if I go in with you."

"Hey now," I said, giving him a playful jab. "You said you were done with the misguided chivalry."

He at least had the good grace to look abashed. "Sorry. Old habits and all that. I'll leave you to it." He squeezed my hand before rising back up the stairs and locking the trapdoor behind him. I waited until I heard the clunk of the floor phasing back together above, then passed through the shimmering barrier and into the prison cell.

The four vampire chefs sat side by side on a long bench, each with their hands folded in their laps and wrists bound by magical cuffs that glowed neon.

"Look, as we've already told your colleagues, we don't know anything," the vampire on the far left muttered, fixing his cold eyes on me.

I'd never interrogated anyone before, but now that I was the most powerful being in existence, I couldn't pass up the opportunity to gain information from this quartet. "Where did you come from? Before you arrived in Beech Grove?"

"Why should we tell you?" It seemed that this vampire had been elected as their collective voice.

I paced the small prison hold until I was standing directly in front of him. Then I closed my eyes and focused on what I wanted to happen. I imagined the vampire readily and truthfully answering my questions, then held that image in my brain as I asked again. "Where did you come from?"

"Blueberry Bay. In Maine," he offered at once.

Whoa, that was almost too easy.

"I've been there," I said. This time I focused on the undulating magic inside me, how it comforted and calmed, then pushed that feeling out toward the vampire seated before me.

He visibly relaxed, loosening his posture and slowing his breaths. "We know. That's how we first learned of you. That's why we came."

"The four of you and Vanessa?"

"No, our boss."

"Who's your boss?"

"We don't know."

"Did Vanessa know?"

"No. We only know the people at our level and directly above. Leadership remains a secret to protect the cause."

"What is the cause?"

He hesitated, turning his face away from mine.

"What is the cause?" I repeated, imagining him giving me the answer and then immediately following up with my calming magical touch.

The captive vampire's face contorted in a quickly flashing array of emotions—rage, temptation, sorrow, remorse. Still he didn't speak.

But the vampire beside him did. "To unite the world under one magic. One power."

"A global dictatorship?"

"To his power," all four vampires chimed as one.

"Whose?"

"We don't know," the first answered again.

I sighed. "Ah, yes, the layers of leadership." Whoever was in charge had clearly prepared for this scenario. Our prisoners couldn't talk if they didn't even know anything.

"Why do you want to unite the world? What's in it for you if you won't even be the one in charge?"

"We will—" the second began.

"Silence!" the first vampire cut him off with a growled warning.

"We've already said too much."

"I can't resist," the other moaned. He began to shake violently as if having a seizure.

"Then you know what we must do. What we all must do."

I watched in horror as all the vampire captives began to scream and shake until one by one they slumped over.

"What's happening in here?" Connie cried as she, Parker, and Fluffikins wrenched the trapdoor open and charged down the long flight of stairs.

"I... I don't know."

Fluffikins jumped up onto the first vampire's lap and pawed at his chest. "My word. I've heard of this, but I've never seen it."

"What happened?" Parker asked, moving to my side.

"I was asking them questions, and then all of a sudden, they screamed and shook and passed out."

"They're dead." Fluffikins confirmed what I'd already guessed.

"But how? I thought a stake was the only way to..."

"The heart," the cat mumbled. "Destroy the heart, destroy the magic."

"They used their superior strength to crush their own hearts. You must have been very close to getting answers," Connie said, regarding me warily.

"Barnes, come with me," Fluffikins shouted, jumping off the dead vampire's lap and scurrying toward the stairs. I sent him a silent note of thanks. If Parker had asked me too many questions about what happened here, I doubted I'd be able to answer them while maintaining my Terran secret.

Parker dutifully followed the cat boss, leaving me and Connie alone in the basement prison.

"Has the cat told you what you are?" she asked, looking me up and down.

I summoned the pink, sparkly world magic to my fingertips, and it unfurled, taking the shape of a balloon.

"Ah, there it is," she said dryly. "What were you able to find out before they took their own lives?"

"They came here for me," I whispered, wishing the answer had been different.

Connie frowned. "Yes, that much is obvious."

"You were all in danger, because of me. I can't —" I shook my head when my voice cracked. Was I really something so terrible that these vampire henchmen would rather die than have a discussion?

Connie grabbed me by the shoulders and shook. Hard. "Whatever stupid thing you're thinking right now, remember this. We'll be in much more danger if the bad guys get ahold of you. Right now the best thing we can do is keep you safe and out of their reach. Well, actually, I suggested we kill you and save ourselves a world of problems, but Fluffikins won't allow it."

Then I owed the little black cat my life, it seemed. That is, if I could even die. That would definitely be an important question to ask the next time he and I had a heart-to-heart.

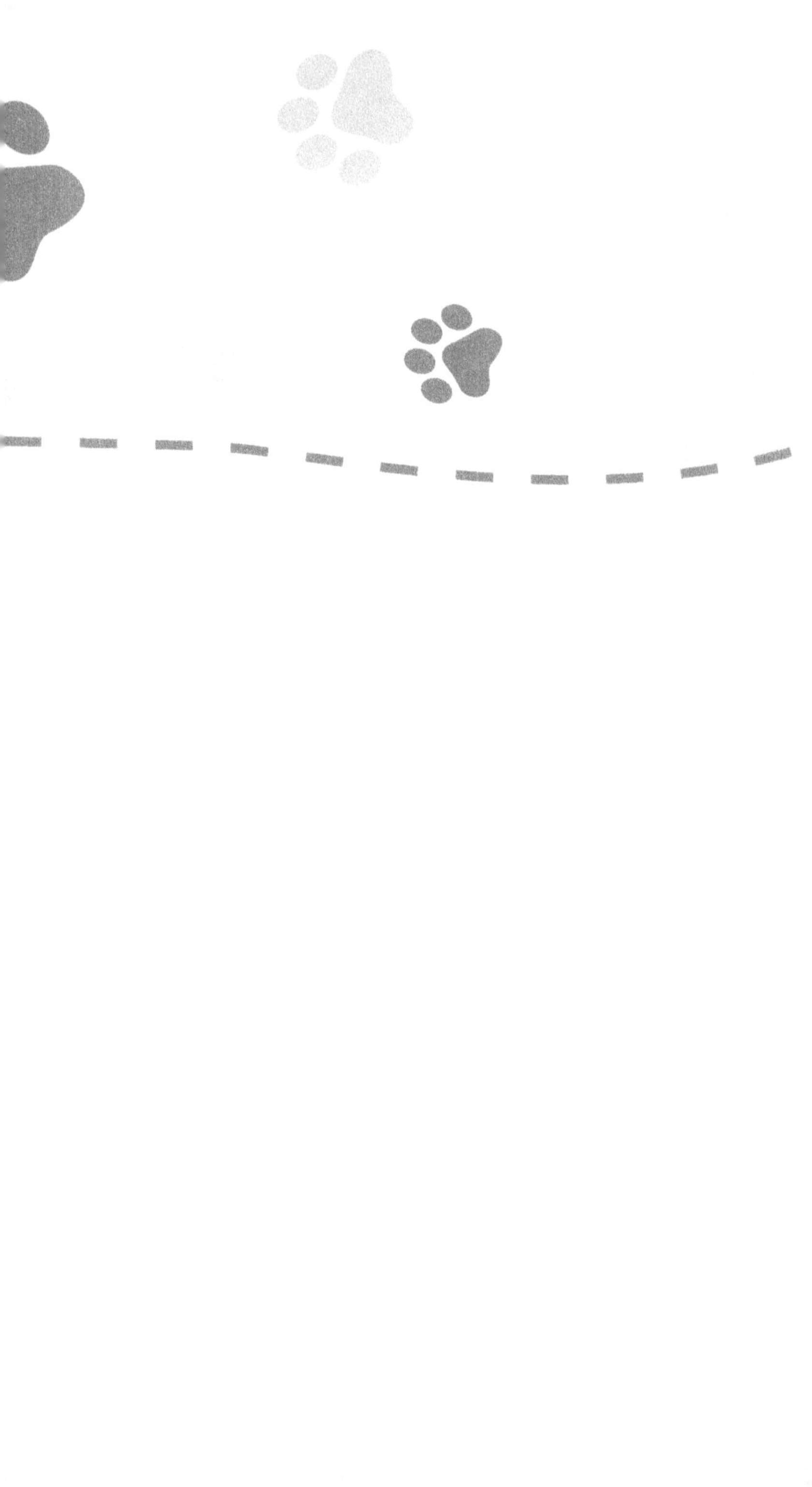

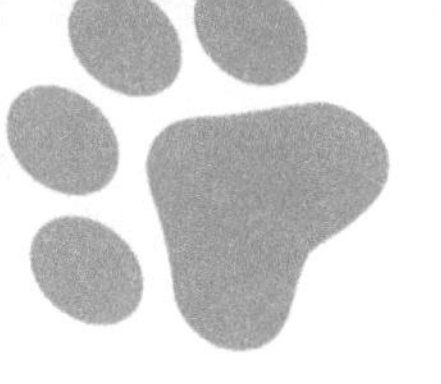

26

"Did you really want to kill me?" I asked, not sure if I was surprised.

Connie's face lit with a cruel smile. "Yup, and I'd have done it myself, too. I still might if you become too much of a handful."

I'd seen Connie stake Vanessa without a moment's hesitation or regret. Still, I'd like to think it would mean something to kill someone she'd known and worked with.

"You hate me that much?" I asked pointedly.

"How many times have we been over this?" the vampire snarled and pointed emphatically toward herself. "Cursed. Remember?"

I leaned against the wall with a heavy sigh.

"You're the only person I can be my real self with. It would be nice to get to know you."

"Fluffikins—"

"Is a cat," I interrupted with a scowl. "And our boss."

"If you think this shared secret will suddenly make us best friends, you're wrong."

"I know all about the vampire curse, but I also know I can overcome it."

Connie's eyes shot to my face and she opened her mouth without speaking, then shook her head and chuckled. "No. I'll believe that when I see it."

"Then come here, and let me show you."

Connie stepped out of the shadows and toward the well-lit staircase.

I followed. "Are you sure about this?" I asked, flexing my fingers in preparation.

She thought about it for such a long while, I wondered if I'd lost her. Finally, she tilted her head thoughtfully and regarded me with cold, black eyes. "I don't want to be a normie again, but it would be nice to feel, to love."

"Do you remember what it's like? Any of those things?" I'd already started to forget during the short time I carried the curse. I couldn't imagine what it was like for Connie to shoulder that burden for so many endless years with no promise of reprieve.

"It's been so long." She closed her eyes and sucked in a deep breath through her nostrils, one we both knew she didn't need.

I shrugged. "You don't have to tell me, if you don't want."

"Yes, but you'll keep asking. I might as well save myself the annoyance."

I waited in silence until she spoke again.

When she did, her voice came out at a strange cadence. "When I was mortal, I fell in love with an angel named Symont. Supernaturals didn't have to hide in those days. The Terrans reigned and kept all species living in easy harmony. Symont and I enjoyed many blissful years together. Unfortunately, I aged normally while he hardly grew any older at all. I developed crow's feet and smile lines, but he remained the perfect picture of youth. Forty might not seem old these days, but many centuries ago it was quite the advanced age. My love couldn't stand to lose me, so he sought for a way to give me immortality so we could always be together."

"So he turned you into a vampire," I murmured.

She straightened to her full height, several inches taller than me. "I chose to become a vampire. It's not like there's any way to turn a mortal into an angel, so I agreed to it as the only possible solution. Once I was transformed, though, Symont hated the monster I had become. Vampires and angels are natural enemies, and what we were proved stronger than what was in our hearts."

"He left you." Even though I knew Connie couldn't feel the sting of this pain from long ago, my heart ached for her.

She fixed her eyes on a spot in the far corner of the room. "Yes. He had no choice. We thought our love could overcome the curse, but we were fools."

"Do you miss him? Are you hoping you might be able to reunite?"

She shrugged and shook her head. "I can't remember. I remember what happened, but I'm completely removed from it. Like it happened to someone else instead of me. As for hope..." She sighed. "How could I ever think that anyone would lift the curse if we couldn't?"

"Fluffikins tells me I am the most powerful person living. And when the world magic entered me, everything came back to me. Maybe I can help you get it back, too. Will you let me try?" I asked, raising my hands and showing off the pink glow surging within.

Connie nodded slowly. "I can't remember how it felt to love, but logically I know it must have been amazing for me to voluntarily turn myself into this... this thing for the chance to preserve it." She reached her hands forward and wedged her fingers between mine.

I still didn't know exactly how my magic worked, but it was something I'd have to learn by myself. Nobody else could tell me exactly what to do. The only way to find out whether I could even lift Connie's curse was to give it a try.

I took several deep breaths and closed my eyes, pushing magic out through my fingers into hers.

The vampire squeezed my hands tight but didn't back away.

I kept moving forward, infusing my magic with love, compassion, humanity—even though neither of us was truly human. And apparently I had never been.

Connie sucked in a sharp breath. "I feel..." she said, but then her words broke off as she sucked in a deep, shaky breath.

I held steady, keeping the connection between

us open but not pushing anything else through to her.

When Connie didn't speak again, I blinked my eyes open just in time to see her collapse lifeless to the ground.

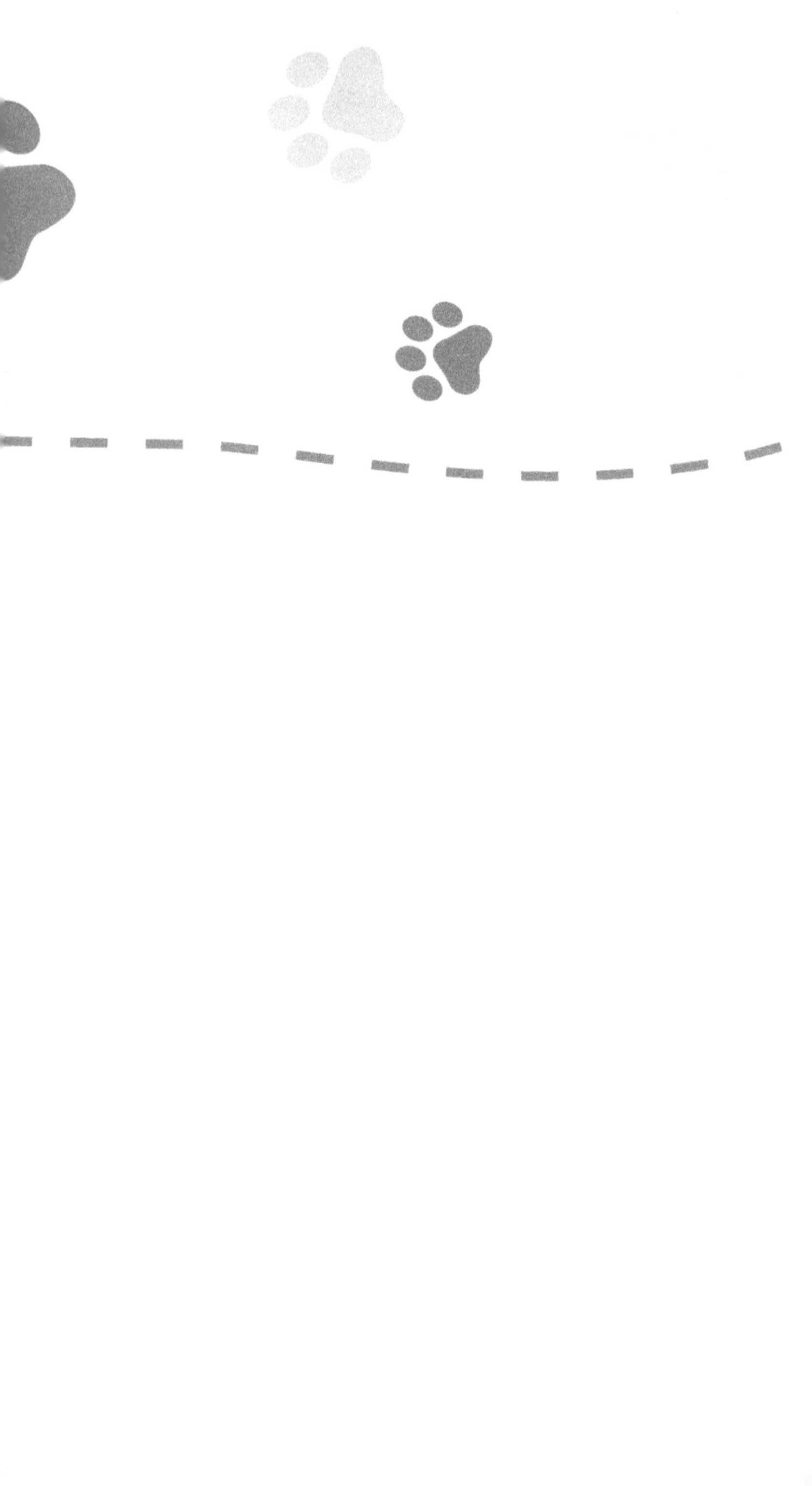

27

dropped to my knees and placed my head to Connie's chest. No heartbeat, but she also hadn't had one before.

"Connie!" I cried out, shaking her shoulders. I was too afraid to use any more of my magic until I learned what had gone wrong here.

When she didn't rouse, I shot the world magic from my fingertips like powerful bolts of lightning, allowing it to form in the air before me.

"Find Fluffikins," I pleaded. "Bring him here."

The sparkling pink swirls united in a long tendril and snaked through the ceiling.

I continued my efforts to revive Connie, but nothing I tried had any effect. *No, no, no!*

I wasn't a killer, and yet five vampires had

dropped dead at my feet in less than fifteen minutes.

"What did you do?" Fluffikins roared, zooming down the steps after taking care to seal the trapdoor behind him.

My magic returned and crashed into me from behind. I drew in a sharp breath from the shock. The suddenness of it hurt. My system had been given no time to adjust to the intense change, and I definitely wasn't adept at controlling my Terran magic yet. Just look at what I'd done to Connie!

At the same time I could tell the magic had craved my touch for a long time. Centuries maybe. Fluffikins had explained that this world magic was as old as the earth itself. It didn't belong to me nor did I belong to it, but we belonged together.

Symbiotic.

My moment of pain was nothing compared to the long years it had been forced to endure without me or others like me. We would figure this thing out.

But first we had to save Connie.

"I tried to lift the curse for her. The same way I did for myself," I told the frantic cat at my side.

"You flooded her with the world magic?" he asked, aghast.

"No, I very slowly fed it into her. I was careful. I—"

"Didn't listen! You didn't listen!" he shouted in my face. "It's too much. Her heart couldn't hold it all. You killed her."

"No!" I shouted. "That's not possible! She's a vampire. She shouldn't have—"

Fluffikins spun and scratched at the ground, sending wave after wave of magic into Connie. Nothing happened.

"I didn't m-mean to," I sputtered as tears splashed across my cheeks.

"You need to learn to control your magic before you use it again," the cat hissed.

"That's enough for today. Return to me," he commanded the magic inside me.

Again nothing happened.

"Return!" the boss cat shouted, spittle flying.

My skin flashed pink, then returned to its normal peach.

"You refuse?" he hissed in rage.

"Not me," I said, trying to summon and expel the magic.

I glowed pink again, but the magic remained where it was.

The magic inside me, it was sentient. It had its own mind, and now it shared my body.

As I realized this, my hand raised of its own volition and came to rest on Connie's chest. I watched my fingers light up as they sunk into the deceased vampire's chest. I felt it, cold and squishy in my hand, Connie's heart.

I cried as my hand clamped around the lifeless organ.

"What are you doing?" Fluffikins demanded in horror.

"I'm not," I said, beginning to hyperventilate, such was my fear.

"Then stop."

"I can't," I cried, even as I tried—and failed—to yank my hand free from Connie's chest.

But then her heart began to beat within my hand. Faint and slow at first, but then faster, stronger.

The magic released me, and I pulled my hand free, gasping and crying when Connie opened her eyes and rose to a sitting position.

"What happened?" she croaked, bringing a hand up to rub at her chest. "Where am I?"

"No, it's not possible." Fluffikins walked back until he bumped into the wall. His wide eyes glowed with what I took to be equal parts fright and respect. Somehow I just knew how others felt now. At least some of the time.

"Are you okay?" I asked Connie breathlessly as my frazzled nerves began to relax again.

"I feel..." she began, echoing the same words she'd spoken just before she'd crumpled in a heap on the ground.

"Alive," she said at last, her eyes blinking rapidly as she studied her arms and chest. "How?"

I opened my mouth to answer, but there was no explanation.

Connie twisted with a grunt and grabbed the wooden stake from the holster at her ankle and dragged it across the soft flesh of her forearm.

"Ahhh!" she cried as deep scarlet blood poured from the wound.

"Alive!" Fluffikins wailed. "Alive! But no one can raise the dead!"

"Tawny did," the vampire said with that familiar smirk of hers, and then she flung her arms around me and sobbed into my hair.

I hesitated. "Are you...?"

"Human again, yes!" She kissed both of my cheeks in such effusive delight that I could scarcely recognize her.

"It's not possible," the boss cat muttered again.

"The curse is gone?" I asked hopefully, hesitantly.

Connie rose to her feet and then laughed when she stumbled back a step. "I'm clumsy. And I can feel. And hurt. And, and… Thank you, Tawny. Thank you so much for freeing me from that life!"

"This is not good," Fluffikins hissed as he ran for the stairs.

Had I done something wrong? The boss cat seemed to think so, but how could saving a life ever be a bad thing?

I let Connie wrap me in her arms and sob into my hair with wave after wave of joy and told myself I'd done something good—even if I hadn't exactly been the one to do it.

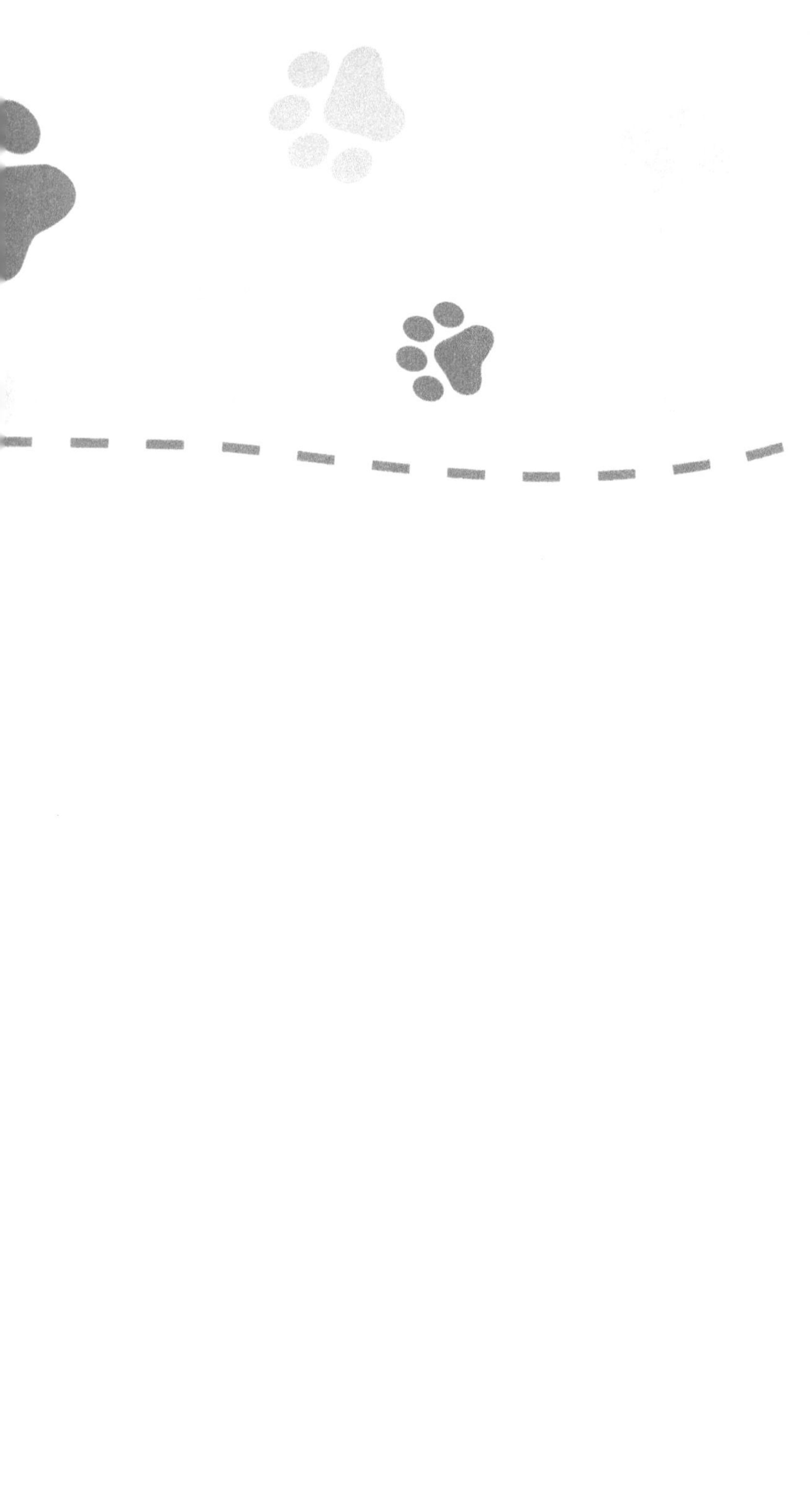

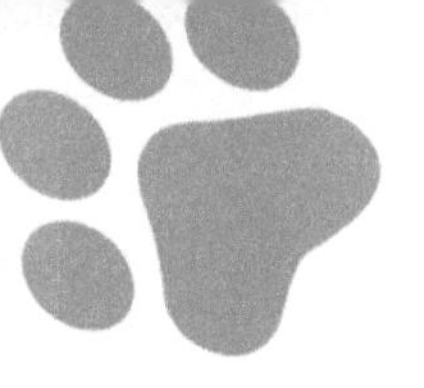

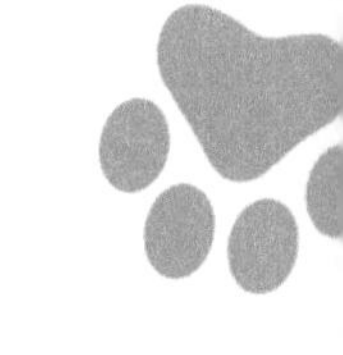

28

"Connie," I cried as a sudden revelation hit me. "If I raised you, I can—"

I turned to the four vampire captives hunched over in the jail cell, and Connie followed my line of sight.

"Raise the others, yes!" she squealed.

"They told me some things before..." I broke off, not wanting to describe the horrific scene I'd witnessed.

"This one." I stopped before the second captive on the bench. "He was going to tell me more before the other stopped him, and then they... you know."

"Can you stop them from doing it again?"

"I don't know. Maybe, but Fluffikins said—"

"Who cares what Fluffikins said. We've got a great chance here. You have to take it."

"He doesn't want me to use my magic again until I'm better at controlling it."

"What's the worst that can happen, though?"

"Well, I killed you."

She broke into a huge toothy—and fangless—smile. "Only a little bit. I'm back now and better than ever."

"Yes, you are," I said with a grateful laugh. We actually would be friends, Connie and I, and—oh—how I'd needed it.

"They're already dead. Raise one, ask your questions. They're all bound and imprisoned. Literally nothing can go wrong with this. You have to do it."

I nodded and flexed my fingers, drawing the magic forward. "It's gross," I warned.

Connie rolled her eyes and blew a raspberry. Wow, it was going to take me some time to get used to the new version of her. "Um, I drank human blood for more than a century until the gilded age came and changed our ways."

"You're not a vampire anymore," I reminded her as a smile quirked at my lips.

"Oh, right!" She smacked a palm into her forehead then let out an oof of pain. "Wow, that's going to take some getting used to."

That's what I had just thought. Well, at least we were on the same page now. I probably would have laughed had I not been dreading what I had to do next.

I sunk to my knees before my subject, closed my eyes, and took three slow breaths in and out before plunging my hand into his chest and grabbing hold of his heart.

When the vampire's heart began to beat within my fist, I kept my hold to prevent him from being able to crush his own heart again. I was reasonably certain that he was now human like Connie, but I didn't want to take any chances.

"What's going on?" the prisoner asked, blinking his eyes open slowly. "What did you do to me? I don't feel right."

"Never mind about that. We were having a nice chat before, and you were just about to tell me your plans for uniting the world under one power."

"Not my plans, his."

"Who is he, this one with the plans?"

"I don't know."

"Then why are you helping him?"

"We will no longer have to live in the shadows. Magicks will openly rule."

"What about the humans?"

"They can submit of their own free will or be forced to do so. He will be good to those who accept his leadership."

"What about the ones who don't?"

"Will be destroyed, naturally."

"And you want this?"

"It doesn't matter what I want. It's about all of us."

"It matters to me. Why are you going along with all this?"

"I'm tired of being made to feel like I shouldn't exist. That my very survival is a sin."

"But isn't that what you want to do to people without magic?"

"No, they will be put out of their misery. Meanwhile I am trapped in mine."

I let go and pulled my hand from his chest. "Thank you."

"What will happen to me now?"

Connie put a hand on my shoulder. "Tawny, go. Let me tie up this last loose end."

"But..." I wanted to argue, to defend this

vampire's life, especially now that he may be mortal again.

"He already made his choice," Connie reminded me. "I'm just setting him back to the way he was. I promise to do so gently."

I shook my head, not wanting to answer either way.

The magic decided for me, carrying me up the steps before I could decide what action I wanted to take.

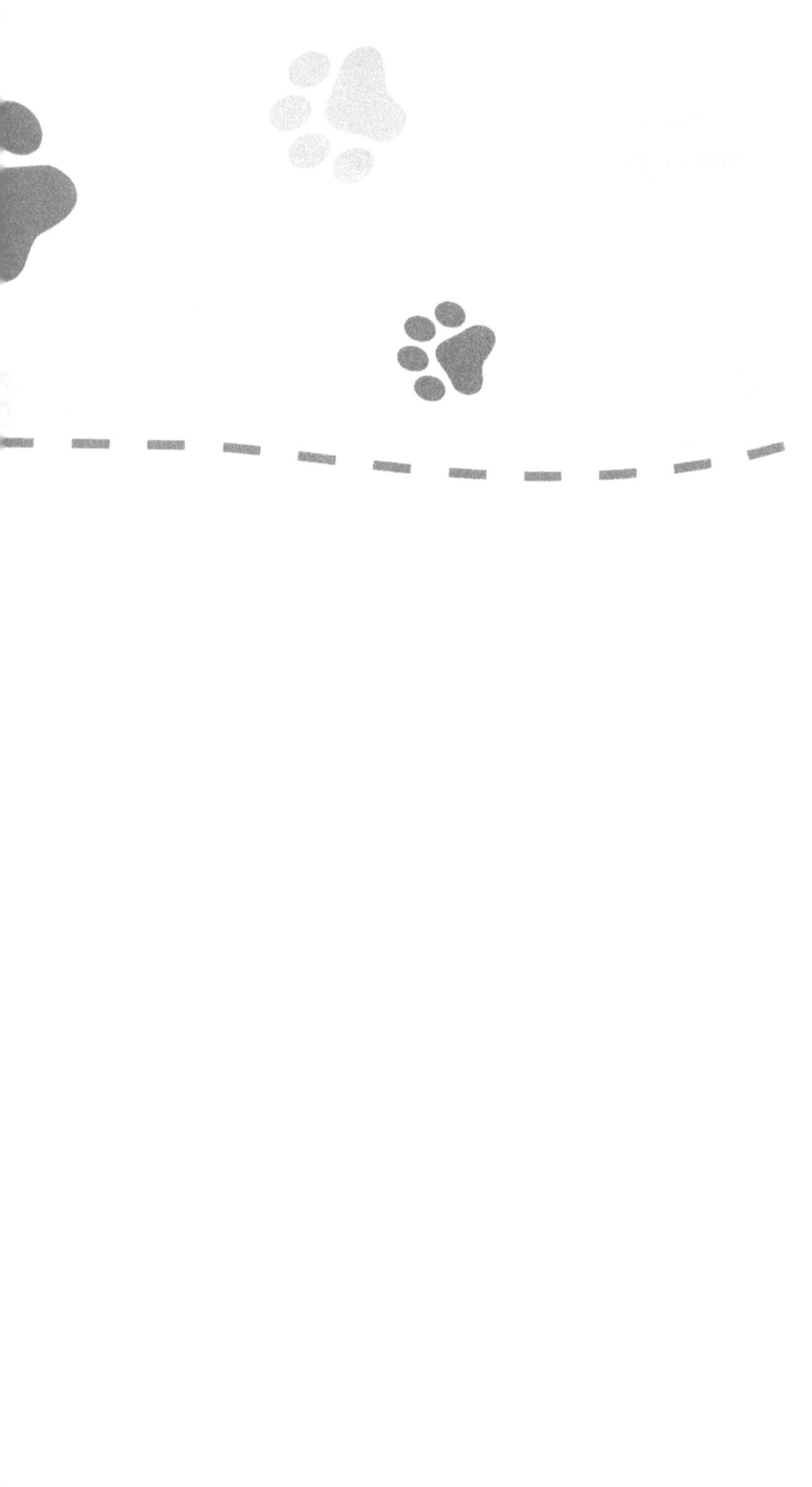

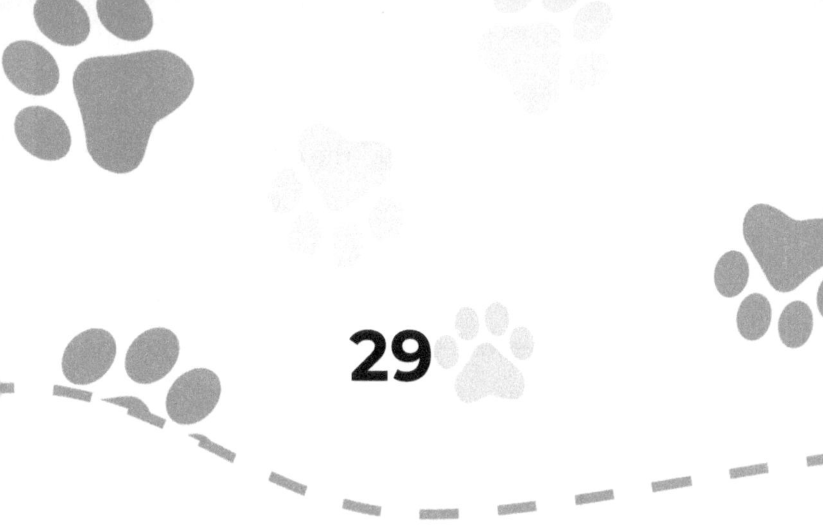

29

Melony stood waiting for me in the warehouse. "C'mon," she said once I emerged from the hidden dungeon. "Everyone's gathering in the conference room. Boss cat told me to get you, so consider yourself got."

I nodded and followed her through the office building and into the glass conference room where the board gathered to discuss its most important business. As soon as I stepped inside, the world magic unspooled from inside me and rose to the ceiling in a thick fog.

"Oh, so now you want to behave," Fluffikins groaned.

"I'm sorry," I murmured, quickly grabbing a chair.

"I wasn't talking to you," the cat snapped, which I took as my cue to sit quietly and wait for whatever news the board had to share.

Connie was the last to join us, not five minutes later. When she took her seat beside me, Fluffikins assumed his war general march up and down the table.

"The rival coven has been dispatched," he revealed, although by now, I assume everyone already knew. "Buckley was able to identify the potion they laced in the food at Bollyweird."

"What was it?" Melony asked, drawing a look of ire from the cat.

"*Verstärker,*" Buckley answered after rising to stand awkwardly before the rest of us. "It's a magical amplifier."

"Why would they feed a bunch of normies a magical amplifier?" Parker wondered aloud.

I'd wondered the same thing silently and found the answer quickly.

Connie squeezed my hand under the table. She and I both knew what the coven had been up to. They'd been trying to draw out other Terrans.

"We can't know," Fluffikins lied to the others without so much as a glance my way. "The good news is that it won't hurt them and doesn't need to be reversed."

"Still, we should follow up," the angel Greta said, offering me a matronly smile.

"I agree," Mr. Fluffikins said with a quick nod. "Which is why I'll be sending Tawny door to door to follow up with all those who dined at Bollyweird before we shut it down."

"Are you sure the normie is the right choice for this assignment? I could have it done faster and better," Melony argued, crossing her arms and slumping back in her chair.

"Yes," the cat said. "Tawny is the right choice, especially considering my next announcement."

All eyes zoomed to me.

Connie kept tight hold of my hand and leaned to whisper in my ear. "They can't know I've changed. Keep my secret if you want to keep yours."

Fluffikins strode over and plopped down in front of me on the table. "During this mission we discovered the most magnificent thing."

"Oh?" Greta offered me a bright, encouraging smile. It seemed so long ago that she offered me her angel armor and ultimately saved my life. I hoped she'd be proud of what I was becoming, even though I was under strict orders never to reveal the truth to her or anyone else.

"Go ahead, Tawny," Parker urged, pointing an equally gigantic grin my way. "Tell them what you told me."

Oh, right.

"I'm not a normie. I'm a witch. Surprise!"

Gasps rose from those who hadn't heard the news yet—either the fake news or the actual discovery Fluffikins had made about me.

"You promised me liaison to the force first!" Melony protested.

"Relax, Haberdash," the cat growled, the fur on his back pricking up. "Your job is safe, even though Tawny will no longer be a temp."

"Is her work with the PTA done?" Greta asked with a pinched brow. She'd rooted for me from day one, and unlike Parker, she'd never doubted that I could make it in this strange new world of magic.

"No, but mine will be soon," the cat announced solemnly.

More gasps.

"As you all know, I'm on my seventh life. I'd like to be able to retire some time during my eighth and enjoy my ninth pursuing the various luxuries available to a cat of my stature. As such, I will be training Tawny as my replacement."

"A diplomat!" R balked, twisting his long beard around his hand pensively. "That's a pretty big promotion."

"Yes, it is," Fluffikins said, keeping his eyes fixed on mine. "But I have full faith that Tawny can handle whatever comes next."

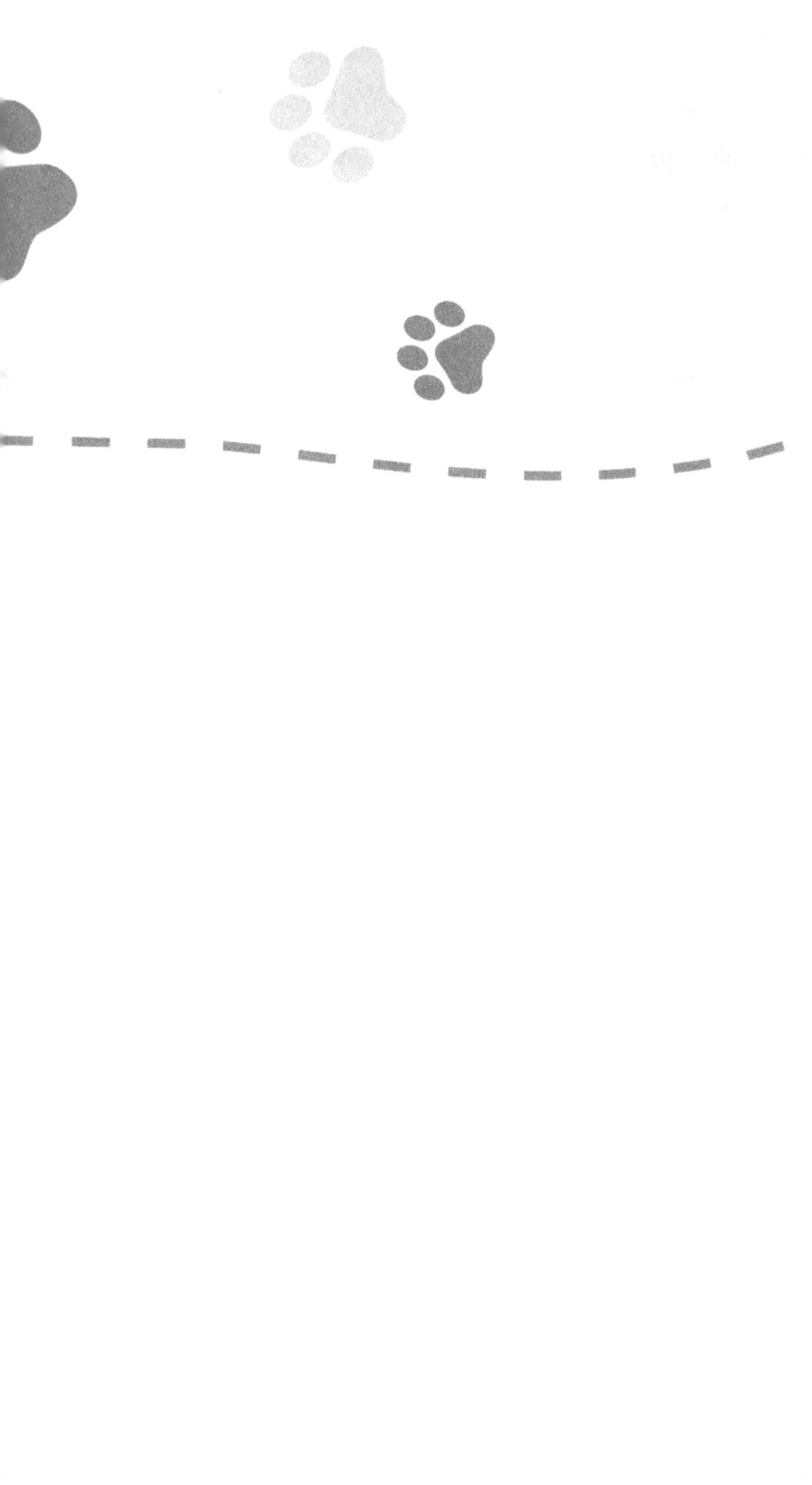

30

So there you have it...

In the span of not even twenty-four hours, I found out that I was the last known member of the most powerful species to ever exist.

I absorbed a strong magical current and found out it was able to control me just as much as I could control it.

I raised the dead, not just once but twice.

The irritating cat boss was revealed to be my biggest supporter all along.

An ornery vampire became my best friend.

I got a fake promotion.

And was directed to keep my true nature a secret from everyone, including Parker.

The two of us officially became an item, of course.

Then there's the wannabe magical dictator who plans to either enslave humanity, destroy it, or both.

And, oh, yeah. I'm the only one who has even a sliver's chance of stopping that from happening...

When this all started, I was just a part-time romance novelist turned paranormal temp.

And now I'm the one person who can either save the world or end it.

No pressure, right?

You didn't think it was over, did you? Tawny and the gang will be back soon.

———

Pssst... If you absolutely loved this book and want even more, make sure you **sign up for Molly's newsletter**. When you do, you'll receive an exclusive digital prize pack, including a free book!

WHAT TO READ NEXT!

My name is Gracie Springs, and I am not a witch... but I'm pretty sure my cat is. I first started to get suspicious when he jumped just a little too high while chasing after a robin in our front yard. I knew for sure when he opened up his mouth and addressed me by name!

The first thing he told me? That he doesn't like the name I gave him—even though "Fluffy" fits him like a warm sweater at Christmas. Now we've compromised on "Merlin the Magical Fluff," which according to him references his long and proud lineage just fine.

After that small matter was settled, he informed me that I must uphold his secret or risk spending the rest of my life in some magical prison. I agreed, not knowing it would turn into a full-time job of covering his tracks and fibbing our way out of some pretty tight spots.

When my boss at the local coffee shop turns up dead as a dormouse, things go from challenging to practically impossible... especially since all my coworkers seem to think I'm to blame.

Here's hoping my witchy cat can charm our way out of this one, because right now it looks like I'm cursed if I do and charged with murder if I don't. Yikes!

MERLIN TAKES A FAMILIAR is now available.

Get your copy so that you can start reading this zany mystery series today!

My name is Gracie Springs, and I've always been a pretty normal girl. I work as a barista while working toward my master's degree in Sociology. I've finished all my coursework but still haven't landed upon the perfect thesis topic. And I can't earn my degree until I do.

Oops.

Meanwhile I live in a small suburban town in Southern Georgia called Elderberry Heights. And the name fits it to a *T,* because most of my neighbors are somewhere north of seventy years old. I'm living in my grandma Grace's house, which she left behind when she chose to move south to a trendy retirement community in the Florida Keys.

She gave me the home where she raised my

father and all my uncles, saying it was my early inheritance and that I'd always been her favorite, anyway—and not just because we shared a name.

She left all her furniture and decor, which means my house has at least three dozen hand-crocheted doilies and the living room is made up of brown floral couches and honey oak side tables. I don't have the heart—or the money—to change anything.

Grandma Grace also left me this ragamuffin cat that turned up at her doorstep only days before she'd been scheduled to move out and me to move in. The vet says he's a Maine Coon. I say he's much larger than any cat should ever be, especially considering all that stripey fur that poofs out from his body and makes him look like a literal fluff ball.

I guess that's why I named him Fluffy.

Keeping a cat I hadn't wanted was a small price to pay for being handed a free house, and over time Fluffy has started to grow on me. He's not exactly the cuddly type. In fact, every time, I've tried to pick him up, he's gone for blood. And succeeded in getting it twice.

I don't try to pick him up anymore, but if I sit really still and pretend I'm not interested, sometimes he'll help himself to my lap. Once he even purred.

Fluffy does love food and often takes a bite of whatever I'm having for dinner. He also enjoys running up and down the hallways in the middle of the night like a creature possessed.

I hadn't meant for him to be an outdoor cat, but he's such a good escape artist that eventually I just installed a pet door so I wouldn't have to worry about it, anymore.

That brings me to this morning...

I was running late for work, thanks to having a particularly difficult time following a new makeup tutorial from my favorite beauty Tuber. In the end, I scrubbed off the whole thing and went with a smoky eye and nude lip. That'd teach me to try something new so close to the start of my shift.

Especially since my mean old boss would take any excuse to dock my pay. He's still bitter that a popular franchised cafe moved in a couple streets away and cut his profits considerably. But he's also stubborn and not quite ready to admit defeat, which is why he's kept the whole staff on while slashing our hours and looking for any excuse to pay us less.

Great guy, that boss of mine.

I hadn't seen Fluffy since breakfast and wanted

to make sure everything was okay with him before taking off for my shift.

"Fluffy! Fluffy! Here, kitty, kitty!" I called and clicked my tongue, but he didn't come running. He never comes running. It's always up to me to find him.

And so I looked under the bed, behind the couch, and out the front window.

Finally I spotted him with his butt in the air and face toward the ground in that classic pre-pounce pose. Across the way stood an unaware robin bathing in the stone birdbath Grandma left behind with whatever few drops hadn't yet been evaporated by the hot summer sun.

Wiggle, wiggle, went Fluffy's butt.

He leaped, but the robin saw him coming and flittered away.

Fluffy flittered after him.

Not just a normal cat leap, either. He looked like a tiny feline athlete about to slam dunk a basketball. Up and up he went after that frightened avian target. He must have gone at least six feet into the sky and was still climbing up, up, up.

That's when he turned his head my way and saw me watching. Those emerald eyes bored straight into mine, and for a moment he remained stuck mid-jump just hanging in the air.

Then he turned again, and the sudden movement broke the spell. Fluffy came crashing straight back to earth, then skittered out of sight, leaving me to wonder: *What in the heck just happened?*

———

I chalked the whole gravity-defying cat episode up to poor sleep and an overactive imagination, then hurried my way over to Harold's House of Coffee.

Despite ignoring both speed limits and stop signs, I wound up three minutes late for my shift. My boss, Harold himself, stood just inside the front door waiting for me.

He tapped his wrist even though he never wore a watch and shouted, "When will you learn? Three minutes means three dollars, and since this is your second offense this week, I'm doubling it."

I snorted and rushed past him to clock in.

"Gracie! Aren't you listening to me?" he demanded, trailing after me like a demented duckling.

"Yes, you're docking me six dollars for being three minutes late, even though we have no customers and you only pay us minimum wage. And even that's because you're legally obligated. Pretty soon I'm going to be paying you for the pleasure of standing around with nothing to do while our customers hang out at Mermaid's Brew down the street. Does that sound about right?"

Harold's face turned bright red. "The insolence!" he screamed. "If it didn't cost so much to train someone new, you'd be out of a job. In fact you're lucky that I—"

He took a step back, shook his head, and tried again. "Listen here, Gracie. You're lucky that—"

His words stopped coming as he gasped and crumpled to the floor. From hotheaded to out cold in mere seconds.

"Harold, Harold!" I cried and fell to my knees to check if he was breathing.

He wasn't.

I grabbed his wrist and tried to find a pulse.

I couldn't.

Ruh-oh.

**MERLIN TAKES A FAMILIAR is now
available.**

***Get your copy so that you can start reading this
zany mystery series today!***

ABOUT MOLLY FITZ

While *USA Today bestselling* author Molly Fitz can't technically talk to animals, she and her three feline writing assistants have deep and very animated conversations as they navigate their days.

She lives with her child and their own private zoo somewhere in the wilds of Alaska. Molly will occasionally venture out for good food, great coffee, or to meet new animal friends.

Learn more about Molly and her books, and be sure to sign up for her newsletter at **www.Molly Mysteries.com**.

ALSO BY MOLLY FITZ

Learn more about Molly's collected works, so that you can decide which book you'd like to read next...

PET WHISPERER P.I.

Angie Russo just partnered up with Blueberry Bay's first ever talking cat detective. Along with his ragtag gang of human and animal helpers, Octo-Cat is determined to save the day... so long as it doesn't interfere with his schedule.

Start with book 1, ***Kitty Confidential***.

MERLIN'S MAGICAL MYSTERIES

Gracie Springs is not a witch... but her cat is. Now she must help to keep his secret or risk spending the rest of her life in some magical prison. Too bad trouble seems to find them at every turn!

Start with book 1, ***Merlin Takes a Familiar***.

PARANORMAL TEMP AGENCY

Tawny Bigford's simple life takes a turn for the magical when she stumbles upon her landlady's murder and is recruited by a talking black cat named Fluffikins to take over the deceased's role as the official Town Witch for Beech Grove, Georgia.

Start with book 1, ***Witch for Hire***.

THE MYSTERIES OF MOONLIGHT MANOR (WITH TRIXIE SILVERTALE)

Sydney Coleman has it all—until she doesn't. No sooner does she launch her bed and breakfast, than a trio of ghosts turn up oppose her at every turn. They insist she solve the murder of their mistress, but Sydney is desperate for cash. If she can't book some guests fast, her haunted mansion is utterly doomed.

Start with book 1, ***Moonlight & Mischief***.

CONNECT WITH MOLLY

Sign up for my newsletter and get a special digital prize pack for joining, including an exclusive story, *Meowy Christmas Mayhem*, fun quiz, and lots of cat pictures!

Sign up: **MollyMysteries.com/subscribe**

Now, if you ever wished you could converse with cats, here's your opportunity! This is me officially inviting you into my whacky inner world as part of my Cozy Kitty Book Club.

For those who just can't get enough of my zany cat characters and their hapless humans, this book club will provide new content to devour and the chance to get to know my best author friends.

From exclusive stories, behind-the-scenes trivia to never-before-released bonus content, and monthly giveaways, there's a lot to love about the Cozy Kitty Book Club. Join today to find out what we're reading next!

Join: **MollyMysteries.com/club**